THE RESTLESS EARTH

MOUNTAINS AND VALLEYS

THE RESTLESS EARTH

THE RESTLESS EARTH

MOUNTAINS AND VALLEYS

Carolyn Arden

 THE FRANKLIN INSTITUTE

 CHELSEA HOUSE PUBLISHERS
An imprint of Infobase Publishing

MOUNTAINS AND VALLEYS

Chelsea House
An imprint of Infobase Publishing
132 West 31st Street
New York NY 10001

Library of Congress Cataloging-in-Publication Data
Arden, Carolyn.
  Mountains and valleys / Carolyn Arden.
     p. cm. — (Restless earth)
  Includes bibliographical references and index.
  ISBN 978-0-7910-9707-6 (hardcover : acid-free paper) 1. Mountains—Juvenile literature. 2. Valleys—Juvenile literature. 3. Plate tectonics—Juvenile literature. I. Title. II. Series.
  GB512.A73 2009
  551.43'2—dc22   2008027079

Chelsea House books are available at special discounts when purchased in bulk quantities for businesses, associations, institutions, or sales promotions. Please call our Special Sales Department in New York at (212) 967-8800 or (800) 322-8755.

You can find Chelsea House on the World Wide Web at
http://www.chelseahouse.com

Text design by Erika K. Arroyo
Cover design by Ben Peterson

Printed in the United States of America

Bang EJB 10 9 8 7 6 5 4 3 2 1

This book is printed on acid-free paper.

All links and Web addresses were checked and verified to be correct at the time of publication. Because of the dynamic nature of the Web, some addresses and links may have changed since publication and may no longer be valid.

Contents

▲ ▲ ▲

What Is a Mountain?

▲ ▲ ▲

"The end of the ridge and the end of the world . . . then nothing but that clear, empty air. There was nowhere else to climb. I was standing on the top of the world."

—Stacy Allison, first American woman to reach
the summit of Mount Everest

FEW MOUNTAINS ARE SPOKEN OF WITH SUCH AWE AS MOUNT EVEREST, and for good reason: It is the highest place on Earth and also one of the deadliest. For every 50 climbers who make it to the top, one dies. The **summit** of Everest rises up to 29,035 feet (8,850 meters, or m). That is nearly as high as a jet flies and taller than 23 Empire State Buildings stacked up.

It is unnatural for humans to be at such a high **altitude**. There is about a third less oxygen in the air than at **sea level**, and the sun's burning rays are far more powerful. **Altitude sickness**, caused by a lack of oxygen in the blood, can strike anyone who lingers too long in what climbers call the "death zone," at an altitude of 26,247 feet (8,000 m) or higher. Most climbers must breathe bottled oxygen to get to the summit. Temperatures and

At age 71, Katsusuke Yanagisawa, a retired schoolteacher from Japan, became the oldest person to reach the top of Mount Everest, the world's tallest mountain. Climbing Everest is treacherous for even the most experienced mountain climbers and requires special equipment such as oxygen masks.

wind chills in the death zone are so low, **frostbite** quickly develops in exposed skin. Many people have lost fingers, toes, and even the tips of their noses to Mount Everest. High winds can literally blow a climber off the mountain. Others die by slipping on ice and falling. Still, despite all these dangers, every year hundreds of people try to make it to the top of the world.

WHERE THE SNOW NEVER MELTS

The taller a mountain is, the colder it is at the top. For every 1,000 feet (305 m) of altitude, air temperature drops about 3°F. If it is 70°F (21°C) at the base of a 20,000-foot (6,096 m) mountain, it will be 10°F (-12.2°C) on the summit. In July, the highest the temperature gets on the summit of Mount Everest is 0°F (-18°C); in the winter, temperatures can drop to -76°F (-60°C).

The **peaks** of most of the world's tallest mountains are above the **snow line**, the altitude above which snow does not melt. This is why so many tall mountains are snow-capped even in the

Mount Kilimanjaro is the tallest mountain in Africa. It remains snowcapped year round because its summit is above the snow line.

summer. The snow line is at different altitudes in different parts of the world, depending on the local climate.

Even though it is located close to the equator, there is snow on top of Tanzania's Mount Kilimanjaro because it rises 19,340 feet (5,895 m) from the flat African **plains**. From base to summit, Mount Kilimanjaro's environment changes five times: from farmland, to rain and cloud forest, to heath and moorland, to alpine desert, to **glacier**.

Frozen Forever:
Lost on Mount Everest

There are lots of stories about Mount Everest, but one of the most famous is that of George Mallory and Andrew Irvine, two British climbers who disappeared while climbing to the summit in 1924.

On June 6, 1924, **mountaineer** and schoolteacher George Mallory, 37, and engineering student Andrew Irvine, 22, hoped to be the first to stand on top of the world's highest mountain. They had made it to 26,700 feet (8,138 m), where they would leave their camp and start the final and difficult climb to the summit. On June 8, a **geologist** spotted the climbers—looking like two black dots—close to the summit and "going strong." But a few hours later, thick clouds swirled over the mountain, obscuring the view of the peak.

Mallory and Irvine were never seen again.

For decades, their fate remained a mystery. Did they get to the top? Did they fall? Did they run out of oxygen? None of these questions could be answered because their bodies were never found.

Then, in 1999, a special expedition was launched to look for clues to their disappearance. At nearly 27,000 feet (8,230 m) on the North Face of Mount Everest, a grim discovery was made. The frozen

MOUNTAINS STAND TOGETHER

Mount Everest is part of the Himalaya **mountain range**—a wall of rugged, snow-covered peaks 1,500 miles (2,415 kilometers) long bordering northern India and China. The 10 highest mountains in the world are found in the Himalayas, which translates from Sanskrit to "abode of snow."

A mountain range is a group of individual mountains that form a line. For example, Mount Washington, the highest peak in

body of a climber lay facedown in the snow. The body was remarkably well preserved, with 1920s-style clothing and hobnailed boots. Inside a pouch around his neck was a letter addressed in elegant script to "Mr. George Leigh Mallory."

Mallory's frozen body had turned almost pure white. His leg was broken and his arms were stretched uphill, his fingers clawing into the rocks as if he were trying to stop sliding.

Irvine's body was nowhere to be found. The expedition team gathered artifacts from Mallory's corpse and covered it with stones, putting the famous mountaineer to rest 75 years after he died trying to fulfill a dream.

Mallory's is not the only frozen body on Mount Everest. Nearly 200 people have died on the mountain since 1921. Most of their bodies are left on the mountain where they fell. It is dangerous enough to try to climb the mountain; to bring a body back down is next to impossible.

It is still unknown whether Mallory and Irvine died on their way up to the summit, or on the way back down. On future expeditions, researchers hope to recover a camera that Mallory had borrowed the day he and Irvine left camp for the summit. Although the film would be more than 80 years old, it could produce the missing clues to what happened on top of Mount Everest on June 8, 1924.

New Hampshire, is part of the Presidential Range, which is part of the White Mountains chain. A mountain range can be very long or relatively short. The Transantarctic Mountains range in Antarctica is 2,200 miles (3,542 km) in length. The Teton Range in Wyoming is only 40 miles (64 km) long.

Mountains can stand alone, too. Mount Kilimanjaro is a single **volcanic mountain** that rises up over the flat, dry African plains in Tanzania.

MOUNTAINS COME IN DIFFERENT SHAPES

Mountains are built up slowly, over millions of years, by forces deep within the Earth. Geologists recognize four general categories of mountains, based on the forces that shaped them. They are folded, volcanic, dome, and fault-block mountains.

The Himalayas are **folded mountains**, made when the continents of India and Asia collided tens of millions of years ago. Folded mountains are created when pressure causes the Earth's **crust**, or outermost layer of rock, to buckle and fold into ridges and **valleys**, like wrinkles in a thick towel. Some of the most spectacular mountain ranges in the world—including the Alps in Europe, the Urals in northern Russia, and the Andes mountains in South America—are folded mountains.

The peaks of volcanic mountains look very different from those of folded mountains. They are more rounded and symmetrical, with gently sloping sides. Volcanic mountains are formed by vents in the Earth that allow **magma**, or hot, molten rock, to reach the surface, cool, and harden into solid rock. Mount Fuji in Japan, Mount Kenya in Africa, and Mount Rainier in Washington are all volcanic mountains. The Hawaiian Islands are the tops of volcanic mountains that formed on the Pacific Ocean floor.

The gently rolling Black Hills of South Dakota are **dome mountains**. Dome mountains are made when pockets of hot **lava** are trapped underground and heat and pressure force rock layers up into a dome, like a bubble in a pot of boiling soup.

The tallest mountain in the Black Hills is Harney Peak, with an altitude of 7,242 feet (2,207 m). Mount Everest is four times taller!

The Hawaiian Sea Monster

What is the tallest mountain on Earth? If you are thinking Mount Everest, you are only partly right. Mount Everest is the tallest mountain in terms of altitude, but the tallest mountain on Earth from base to summit is actually out in the middle of the Pacific Ocean. It is Mauna Kea, a volcanic mountain we know as the Big Island of Hawaii, named "white mountain" for its snow-capped peaks.

Mauna Kea rises 33,500 feet (10,200 m) from the bottom of the Pacific Ocean. That is almost 5,000 feet (1,524 m) taller than Mount Everest. Only 11,000 feet (3,353 m) of Mauna Kea is above the surface of the ocean; the other 22,000 feet (6,706 m) is underwater.

Mauna Kea is a seamount, a volcanic mountain born on the ocean floor. About 800,000 years ago, it began to grow from an outpouring of lava at the bottom of the sea. This is how all of the Hawaiian Islands were formed. It is a dormant, or "sleeping," **volcano** because it has not erupted for 4,500 years, but still could.

Because of its **elevation** and location, Mauna Kea is an ideal spot for stargazing. The Keck Observatory, with 13 working telescopes used by astronomers from 11 countries, is located at the summit.

Mauna Kea's summit is above the snow line in Hawaii, so snow falls there during the winter months. Winds can reach up to 70 miles per hour (113 kilometers per hour) at the summit. Still, some brave souls make the two-hour drive up to the top to try skiing at the only place they can in tropical Hawaii.

Fault-block mountains form along giant cracks, or **faults**, in the Earth—the same faults that cause **earthquakes**. It is earthquakes that make fault-block mountains rise higher and higher as the ground shifts on both sides of a fault. When a tilted block of Earth slides up on one side of a fault, it forms a mountain range with high walls on one side and a gradual slope on the other. The magnificent Tetons in Wyoming, home to the famous Jackson Hole ski area with its challenging, steep slopes, are fault-block mountains.

IT TAKES TIME TO MAKE A MOUNTAIN

Mountains take tens of millions of years to grow. The period during which a group of mountains is built is called an **orogeny**, which comes from the Greek words *oros* (mountain) and *genes* (born). An orogeny begins at the point when volcanic or **tectonic** forces start to build or change the shape of a mountain range, and ends when that activity stops. Some, like the orogeny that formed the Himalayas, are still going on today.

Geologists have identified the major orogenies that created some of the world's most famous mountain ranges. About 250 million years ago, a series of orogenies created the Appalachians in North America, the Massif Central in France, and the Caledonian Mountains in Scotland and Scandinavia. The Alps in Switzerland arose during the Alpine orogeny, 20 million years ago.

Like a house that is renovated over time to add more rooms, a mountain **chain** can grow and change its shape during several orogenies. The Rocky Mountains in western North America were sculpted during the Sonoma (270 to 240 million years ago), the Sevier (140 to 50 million years ago), and the Laramide orogenies (70 to 40 million years ago).

THE FORCES THAT BRING MOUNTAINS DOWN

Almost as soon as a mountain rises up, it begins to wear down. The forces of nature—wind, water, ice, snow, plant growth—pick

Types of Mountains

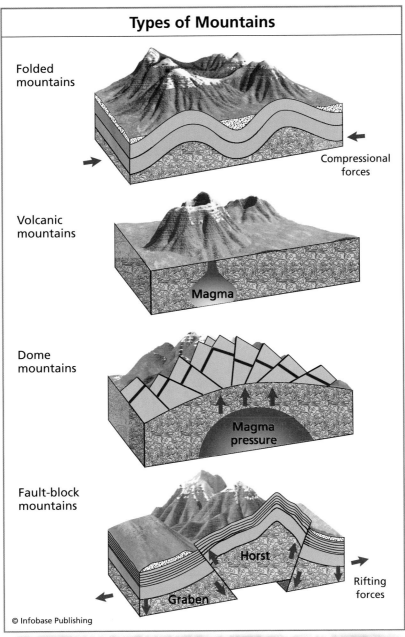

Folded mountains

Compressional forces

Volcanic mountains

Magma

Dome mountains

Magma pressure

Fault-block mountains

Horst

Graben

Rifting forces

© Infobase Publishing

There are four basic types of mountains, identified by the geologic forces that formed them. Volcanic mountains tend to be steeper, with sharper peaks.

away at the rock, carving valleys, lowering peaks, and wearing the mountains down to the ground over hundreds of millions of years. This geological process is called **erosion**.

Younger mountains are usually taller and pointier, with dramatic peaks and steep valleys, while older mountains are lower and rounder, with gently rolling hills and valleys carved by erosion over time.

Mount Everest is the tallest mountain on land today, but it would have had some fierce competition when Earth was relatively young. Geologists have discovered that the very old rocks in an area of eastern Canada, known as the Canadian Shield, were once part of an enormous mountain range with peaks as high as 39,600 feet (12,070 m). Today, the gently rolling landscape of the Canadian Shield is known for its fertile farmland and peaceful lakes.

Some of the oldest mountains in North America are in the Appalachian chain, which runs along the eastern seaboard from Alabama north to Canada and first began to form 480 million years ago. Compared to the tall and majestic Himalayas, the Appalachians are old and stooped. Worn down by more than 100 million years of erosion, their highest peaks are only about 6,000 feet (1,829 m) in elevation. In their younger days, however, the "ancient" eastern Appalachians were closer in height to the soaring western Rocky Mountains of today.

The Appalachians have a violent past that goes back hundreds of millions of years and includes earthquakes, colliding continents, and explosive volcanoes. Like most of the world's great mountains, the Appalachians were born when the earth moved.

How the Land Changes Shape

▲ ▲ ▲

MOUNT EVEREST IS STILL RISING—ABOUT 0.4 INCHES (1 CENTIMETER) each year. At this rate, the mountain could be 2,500 feet (760 m) higher a thousand years from now. That is almost half a mile! Mount Everest keeps growing because the continents of India and Asia, which collided millions of years ago, are still moving toward each other.

How can continents move? This was a question pondered by German scientist Alfred Wegener in the early 1900s, and it eventually led to one of the most important mountain-building concepts in geology: **plate tectonics**.

THE MOVEMENT OF CONTINENTS

Wegener was studying a map of the world when he noticed something strange. The continents of South America and Africa seemed to fit together like puzzle pieces if they were pushed together across the Atlantic Ocean. (Dutch mapmaker Abraham Ortelius had noticed this too, in 1596.)

Wegener looked for other similarities between the two continents. He compared rock structures on the eastern coast of South

America with those on the western coast of Africa. He examined plant and animal fossils from both continents.

He discovered that the rocks and fossils dating back a few hundred million years were almost identical. How could this be? Africa and South America are separated today by the wide Atlantic

Continental Drift

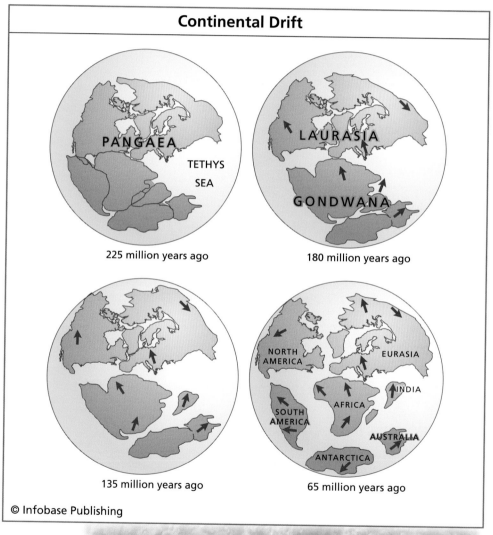

PANGAEA

TETHYS
SEA

225 million years ago

LAURASIA

GONDWANA

180 million years ago

135 million years ago

NORTH
AMERICA   EURASIA

INDIA

SOUTH   AFRICA
AMERICA

AUSTRALIA

ANTARCTICA

65 million years ago

The continents were not always located where they are today. According to the theory of continental drift, they started out together as one huge landmass called Pangaea, then moved slowly over time to their present locations.

Ocean, and their native animals are very different. Sloths, for example, are found in South America, not Africa. Zebras are found in Africa, not South America. The rock and fossil evidence suggested to Wegener that perhaps the two continents were joined together long ago, splitting apart later like a painting that is ripped into two pieces.

Based on this idea, Wegener came up with a bold new theory he called **continental drift**. He proposed that one big supercontinent called **Pangaea** had existed on Earth approximately 225 million years ago. Over time, it broke apart into giant pieces that "drifted" into place to form the world map as we know it today.

PLATE TECTONICS

It would be quite a while before the scientific community would accept Wegener's unusual theory. In 1967, two scientists, W. Jason Morgan of Princeton University in New Jersey, and Dan McKenzie of Cambridge University in England, happened to come up with another theory at about the same time. Known today as **plate tectonics**, it combines continental drift with new findings about the ocean floor to explain how and why the Earth's surface is always changing.

To understand plate tectonics, it helps to visualize what our planet looks like below the surface. If Earth were cut in half like a hard-boiled egg, the yolk would be its solid metallic **core** and the egg white would be the **mantle**—all of the material that lies between the core and the the outermost layer, the crust. It is the crust, the eggshell in our hard-boiled egg model of Earth, that changes shape to form mountains, valleys, and other landscape features.

There are two kinds of crust: continental and oceanic. Continental crust is made of relatively light **minerals** such as quartz and **feldspar** and is 15 to 30 miles thick (24 to 48 km). Oceanic crust is only 3 to 5 miles thick (5 to 8 km) but is made of heavier, dense volcanic rock. Both kinds of crust will break and fold if enough force is applied.

Most of the mantle is hot, molten rock, but the mantle layer just below the crust is cooler and rigid and behaves like solid rock. This mantle layer and the crust that sits on top of it make up what is called the Earth's **lithosphere**. The lithosphere is up to 60 miles (100 km) thick.

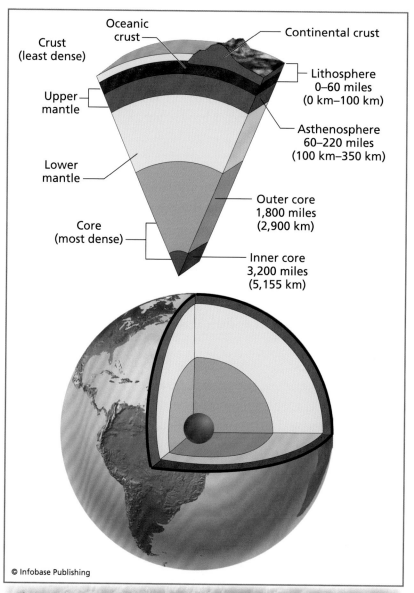

© Infobase Publishing

The Earth is made up of many layers. The thinnest, outermost layer, the crust, is divided into two types: oceanic crust and continental crust. It is the crust that changes shape to form mountains and valleys.

In plate tectonics theory, the lithosphere is broken into giant slabs called **tectonic plates** that fit together like puzzle pieces to cover the globe. There are eight major plates, and several smaller ones. Some plates are so big, they carry more than one continent and parts of oceans, too. For example, the North American plate holds all of North America, Greenland, part of Russia, and portions of the Pacific Ocean, the Atlantic Ocean, and the Caribbean Sea.

The tectonic plates "float" on a mantle layer called the **asthenosphere**, made of hot, thick magma that flows like

Bikinis in Antarctica?

Scientists who do research in Antarctica are a brave bunch. Antarctica is the coldest place on Earth, mostly covered with ice and snow. It holds the world record for the lowest temperature ever recorded on Earth: -129°F (-89°C) on July 21, 1983, at a research station called Vostok. To stay warm, scientists wear lots of layers: thermal underwear, wind pants, flannel shirt, polar fleece, and a big polar parka.

If they had worked in Antarctica about 250 million years ago, they could have worn shorts and bathing suits instead.

By examining rocks and fossils, geologists have discovered that the frozen continent had a tropical past. For example, layers of sandstone located just a few hundred miles from the South Pole contain coal, a deposit that forms in moist, warm climates. Fossils of ferns and trees have also been collected.

In 1969, geologists discovered the fossil bones of *Lystrosaurus*, an ancient reptile about the size of a large dog that lived between 180 and 225 million years ago. Until then, *Lystrosaurus* had only been found in Africa, India, and China.

In 1995, the remains of an armadillolike creature the size of a small car were found, and, in 1998, researchers unearthed a duck-

(continues)

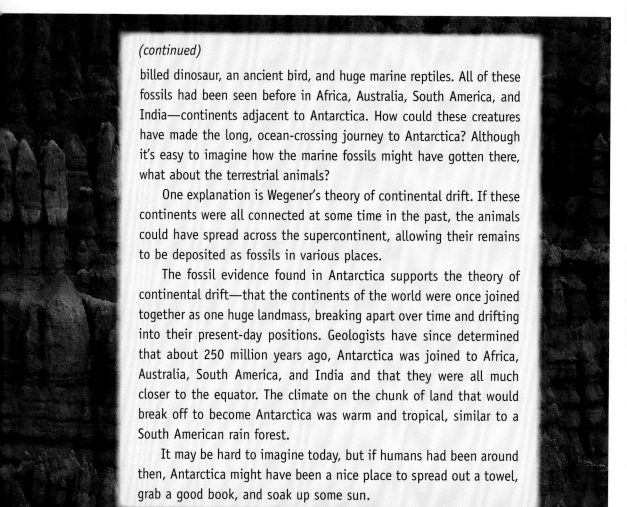

(continued)

billed dinosaur, an ancient bird, and huge marine reptiles. All of these fossils had been seen before in Africa, Australia, South America, and India—continents adjacent to Antarctica. How could these creatures have made the long, ocean-crossing journey to Antarctica? Although it's easy to imagine how the marine fossils might have gotten there, what about the terrestrial animals?

One explanation is Wegener's theory of continental drift. If these continents were all connected at some time in the past, the animals could have spread across the supercontinent, allowing their remains to be deposited as fossils in various places.

The fossil evidence found in Antarctica supports the theory of continental drift—that the continents of the world were once joined together as one huge landmass, breaking apart over time and drifting into their present-day positions. Geologists have since determined that about 250 million years ago, Antarctica was joined to Africa, Australia, South America, and India and that they were all much closer to the equator. The climate on the chunk of land that would break off to become Antarctica was warm and tropical, similar to a South American rain forest.

It may be hard to imagine today, but if humans had been around then, Antarctica might have been a nice place to spread out a towel, grab a good book, and soak up some sun.

warm caramel. Heat circulating from the lower mantle to the asthenosphere and back again, known as convection currents, helps the plates move around like broken crackers in hot soup—slowly sliding past each other, pushing together, and pulling apart.

We cannot see the tectonic plates move any more than we can see a mountain grow. The plates move very slowly, only a few inches per year on average.

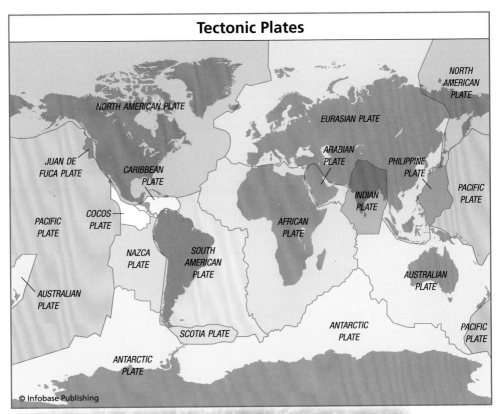

Tectonic Plates

NORTH AMERICAN PLATE

EURASIAN PLATE

ARABIAN PLATE

PHILIPPINE PLATE

JUAN DE FUCA PLATE

CARIBBEAN PLATE

INDIAN PLATE

PACIFIC PLATE

PACIFIC PLATE

COCOS PLATE

AFRICAN PLATE

NAZCA PLATE

SOUTH AMERICAN PLATE

AUSTRALIAN PLATE

AUSTRALIAN PLATE

ANTARCTIC PLATE

PACIFIC PLATE

SCOTIA PLATE

ANTARCTIC PLATE

NORTH AMERICAN PLATE

© Infobase Publishing

The Earth's plates are constantly in motion, although it is too slow to notice. The contact between the plates is what causes mountains to form, volcanoes to erupt, and earthquakes to shake.

PLATE BOUNDARIES: WHERE THE ACTION IS

The seams where plates fit together are called **plate boundaries**. Some plate boundaries are on the ocean floor. Others follow the outlines of continents. The western coast of South America lies along the seam of the Nazca and South American plates, and the western coast of North America lines up with the edge of the Pacific and North American plates.

Two plates can move toward each other, pull apart, or slide past each other. At active plate boundaries, mountains and valleys form, earthquakes rumble, and volcanoes blow. The interactions of the plates over time cause dramatic changes in the Earth's crust.

The Moving Seafloor

When scientists mapped the ocean floor in the 1950s, they discovered an enormous underwater mountain chain. It was more than 31,000 miles (50,000 km) long and more than 1,000 miles (1,600 km) wide, with towering peaks and deep valleys. This chain, called the **mid-ocean ridge**, zigzags around the continents like the stitching on a baseball. All along its length, it is split by a deep **trench**, more than a mile (1.6 km) deep in some places.

The seafloor maps also showed a number of deep, narrow trenches far from the mid-ocean ridge. These other trenches ran parallel to coastal mountain ranges and island arcs. The deepest is the Mariana Trench in the South Pacific Ocean, near Guam. It plunges more than 6 miles (10 km) below the ocean's surface.

U.S. Navy captain and Princeton University geologist Harry H. Hess, who surveyed the Pacific Ocean during World War II, was intrigued by these new findings. Like other geologists, he also wondered why drilling samples had shown that the **sediment** on the

The line of intersection where two plates are moving toward each other is called a **convergent boundary**. If both are continental plates—that is, they carry landmasses—the crust can crumple up into the **folds** of a mountain range.

But when a thinner, heavier oceanic plate meets a thicker, lighter continental plate, the oceanic plate often dives down beneath the other plate. This downward dive is called **subduction**. As the plates keep pushing together, the oceanic plate dives deeper into the Earth, eventually melting and sending hot magma back up to the surface to form volcanic mountains. The Cascade Mountains, on the northwestern coast of the United States, were formed in this way, as were the Andes in South America.

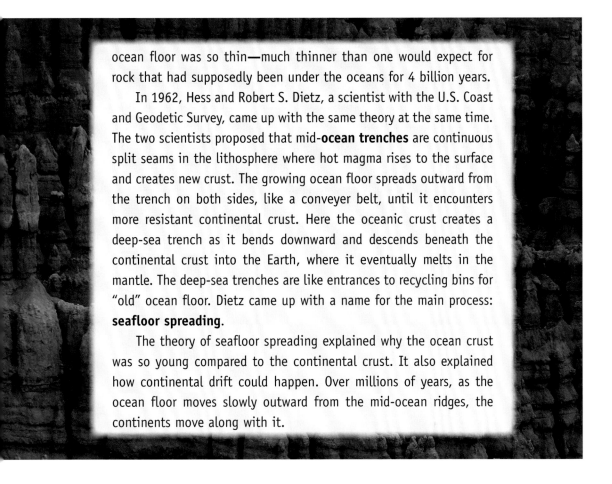

ocean floor was so thin—much thinner than one would expect for rock that had supposedly been under the oceans for 4 billion years.

In 1962, Hess and Robert S. Dietz, a scientist with the U.S. Coast and Geodetic Survey, came up with the same theory at the same time. The two scientists proposed that mid-**ocean trenches** are continuous split seams in the lithosphere where hot magma rises to the surface and creates new crust. The growing ocean floor spreads outward from the trench on both sides, like a conveyer belt, until it encounters more resistant continental crust. Here the oceanic crust creates a deep-sea trench as it bends downward and descends beneath the continental crust into the Earth, where it eventually melts in the mantle. The deep-sea trenches are like entrances to recycling bins for "old" ocean floor. Dietz came up with a name for the main process: **seafloor spreading**.

The theory of seafloor spreading explained why the ocean crust was so young compared to the continental crust. It also explained how continental drift could happen. Over millions of years, as the ocean floor moves slowly outward from the mid-ocean ridges, the continents move along with it.

Volcanoes help scientists pinpoint plate boundaries, since volcanic activity generally happens above the edge of a diving plate or where there is a crack or seam in the lithosphere. The **Ring of Fire** is a circle of active volcanoes that marks the outline of the Pacific plate. It includes volcanoes in Alaska, New Zealand, Japan, Russia, and the northwestern coast of the United States.

The line along which two plates are pulling away from each other is called a **divergent boundary**. In this case, the seam between the two plates allows magma to rise to the surface, creating new crust. As new crust is formed, it is pushed sideways away from the seam, allowing new magma to fill in and create more new crust. As this process continues, it creates the broad, flat valleys of the ocean floors.

A third type of boundary, seen mainly in surface rocks, is a **transform boundary**, where two plates are sliding sideways past one another. This boundary is often marked by a long fracture in the earth called a fault. One of the most famous of these is the San Andreas Fault in southern California. It marks the transform boundary between the Pacific plate and the North American plate, which are grinding past each other at a rate of about 2 inches (5 cm) a year.

Scientists are still trying to make sense of how the plates move and specifically how they change the shape of the Earth's crust. But one thing is certain: The plates are always in motion, causing dramatic changes over time, and sometimes, without warning, an earthquake or **volcanic eruption** on land or under the sea.

3

Folded Mountains
and Volcanoes

▲ ▲ ▲

ACCORDING TO THE THEORY OF CONTINENTAL DRIFT, ABOUT 250 million years ago, when the supercontinent of Pangaea began to split apart, the continental plate carrying India began moving northward at a fast clip of more than 6 inches (16 cm) a year. As the two continents got closer, the floor of the ancient Tethys Sea between the Indian and Eurasian plates shrank and was folded into the rock that would become the mighty Himalayas.

Fossils of marine creatures have been found high on Mount Everest, giving scientists evidence that the rocks that make up the highest mountain on Earth were once at the bottom of a sea.

ROCKS TELL A STORY OF THE PAST
The kinds of rocks found in a mountain tell geologists whether there was volcanic or tectonic activity in its past—or both.

There are three basic kinds of rocks on Earth: **igneous** (volcanic), **sedimentary** (deposited as layers of over time), and **metamorphic**. Igneous rocks include **basalt** and **granite**. Basalt is magma that spills onto the surface under sea or on land and cools rapidly. The ocean floors are made primarily of basalt. Granite is made of magma that has cooled slowly below the Earth's surface, often exposed later in uplifted mountains by erosion, folding, or faulting. Granite is a major component of mountains because so many mountains are formed by volcanic activity. In fact, there is so much granite in the White Mountains of New Hampshire that it is known as the Granite State.

Sedimentary rocks form when layers of deposited material, or sediments, settle one on top of another and harden over time. As more layers settle, the growing pressure of the overlying layers squeezes all the layers together to form hard rock. Sedimentary rocks are important to archeologists and paleontologists because, unlike igneous and metamorphic rocks which are formed under intense heat or pressure, fossils may be preserved in their layers. Limestone, one kind of sedimentary rock, is formed on ocean floors from skeletons of tiny marine animals that are still visible in the rock.

Metamorphic rocks start out as either igneous or sedimentary rocks. Their mineral structure is changed or metamorphosed by high heat or pressure. These transformations take place where continental plates move together or apart, or when rock comes into contact with magma—the same forces that build mountains. Metamorphic rocks are commonly found in mountainous areas and can tell geologists a lot about where a mountain's original rock came from.

Two of the most common varieties of metamorphic rocks found in mountains are **schist** and **gneiss**. Schist is metamorphosed **shale**, a sedimentary rock formed mostly along lakes and rivers. It often contains a purplish-red gemstone called garnet. Gneiss starts out as granite, a common igneous rock, and has a characteristic striping pattern. **Marble** is another metamorphic rock found in mountains. It is made of sedimentary **limestone**. There are many kinds of marble in the world. One of the most famous is Carrara marble from the Apennine mountains of Italy, prized by sculptors for its pure white color and smooth texture.

FOLDS TELL A STORY, TOO

Folded layers of rocks can also give geologists clues to the source and intensity of pressure that created a mountain range. Every rock fold has two parts: the **anticline** is the arch, or top, of the wave; the **syncline** is the bottom, or trough. A single fold can be stretched out over many miles, or it can be only a few yards long.

When part of a mountain is removed, as in the roadcut above, the folds deep within the rock become visible. These folds give geologists important clues to how the mountain was formed.

Folds are visible in the layers of rock, or **strata**, on mountains and along **roadcuts**, where mountains have been sliced through to build roads. Folds can also be seen on the surface as rolling hills and valleys. (A hill is an anticline; a valley is a syncline.)

Geologists include anticlines and synclines in their maps to help them visualize how the crust was deformed over a broad area. The most extreme folds are located close to the point where pressure was applied—for example, at convergent plate boundaries.

Sometimes, the pressure on the rock is so great that folds bend up and over each other. These are called **overturned folds**. The Alps in Europe are famous for their overturned folds, which tell geologists that the mountains were formed by intense horizontal forces—in this case, two converging continental plates (African and Eurasian).

VOLCANIC MOUNTAINS: RISING UP FROM THE DEEP

Folded mountains and metamorphic rocks are created when two plates with continental crust converge. But when continental crust meets oceanic crust, something very different happens. The oceanic plate (made of denser, heavier rock) sinks down, or **subducts,** under the continental plate (made of lighter, airier rock). As it dives down toward the hot mantle, a deep trench forms in the ocean floor, marking the collision zone.

When it gets down to where temperatures are really hot, the leading edge of the oceanic plate begins to melt into magma. This point, where the plate begins to melt, is called the **subduction zone**. Magma made in the subduction zone by the melting oceanic plate finds its way up to the surface through cracks and faults. As it spills out onto the crust, volcanic mountains are made.

The Andes mountains are a good example of this. The vast Andes mountain chain stretches 5,000 miles (8,000 km) along the western coast of South America, crossing through seven countries. This long chain of mountain ranges runs parallel to the

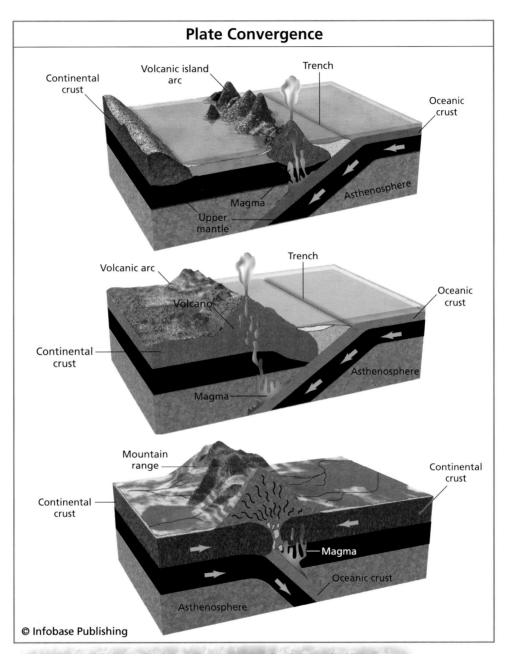

Plate Convergence

Continental crust

Volcanic island arc

Trench

Oceanic crust

Asthenosphere

Magma

Upper mantle

Volcanic arc

Volcano

Trench

Oceanic crust

Continental crust

Asthenosphere

Magma

Mountain range

Continental crust

Continental crust

Continental crust

Magma

Oceanic crust

Asthenosphere

© Infobase Publishing

Folded mountains and volcanoes are made when tectonic plates converge. What happens on the surface depends on the kind of crust that is pushing together. Volcanic mountains form when oceanic crust dives down and melts to form magma; folded mountains rise up when continental crust meets continental crust.

boundary of the oceanic Nazca plate and the continental South American plate—a major subduction zone marked offshore by the Peru-Chile oceanic trench.

Though parts of the Andes mountains started forming approximately 200 million years ago, they are still volcanically active because the Nazca plate is still subducting. Earthquakes are frequent along the western coast of South America, and many of the volcanoes there are still active, which means they could erupt at any time.

When a volcano erupts, it can blow its top off, changing the shape of the mountain by creating a depression, or **crater**, in the top of the cone. After lying *dormant*, or quiet, for nearly 150 years,

Hike Up a Live Volcano!

How would you like to climb to the top of an active volcano and look inside? At Mount St. Helens in the state of Washington, hikers can look down into a crater that has been quietly erupting since October 2004.

Mount St. Helens made big news on May 18, 1980, when a huge eruption triggered by an earthquake blasted off the north face of the dormant volcano, creating a mile-wide (1.6 km) crater. A mushroom-shaped cloud of ash rose 18,000 feet (5,500 m) into the sky and drifted downwind, turning day into night.

David Johnston, a volcanologist with the U.S. Geological Survey, was stationed 6 miles (10 km) from the summit that day. "Vancouver, Vancouver, this is it!" he shouted into his radio as the blast swept toward him at 300 miles per hour (483 kph) with temperatures as high as 660°F (349°C). Trees were snapped like toothpicks, and mudflows destroyed 27 bridges and 200 homes. Johnston was one of at least 57 people killed that day in the most destructive volcanic event in U.S. history.

Mount St. Helens exploded in 1980 and blew ash over hundreds of miles of land, forever changing the shape and environment of the mountain.

When a volcano is extinct, it cannot erupt again because there is no chamber of magma below it. If the top of a volcano has a really big crater, several miles wide, it is called a **caldera**. Beautiful Crater Lake, Oregon, sits in the caldera of an extinct volcano.

Both Mount St. Helens and Crater Lake are part of the Cascade mountain range on the northwestern coast of the United States. This is another subduction zone, where the Juan de Fuca plate is sinking beneath the North American plate.

After the deadly eruption, the mountain was quiet for more than 20 years. Then, in October 2004, a low-level eruption began in the crater, pushing up steam, clouds of ash, and loads of fresh, hot magma. A new lava dome made of ash and rock began to form. Today, visitors to the Mount St. Helens National Volcanic Monument can climb up to the crater's edge, or rim, and look down at the steaming lava dome far below.

It takes about five hours to climb the 8,363 feet (2,549 m) to the rim of the crater. The U.S. Forest Service issues the following warning to anyone who wants to try this hike: "It is very important for all potential climbers to fully understand they may be exposing themselves to volcanic hazards which cannot be forecast, cannot be controlled, and may occur at any time without warning."

So if you want to climb Mount St. Helens, you will need a few extra items in your backpack: a dust mask to block out blowing ash, a helmet to protect against rocks that may be thrown up out of the crater with no warning, and a good sense of balance. After all, it is a drop of more than a thousand feet (305 m) from the rim to the crater floor.

ISLAND ARCS: VOLCANIC MOUNTAINS OF THE SEA

When two oceanic plates converge at the bottom of the sea, volcanic mountains form the same way they do on land. The only difference is that they rise up to become islands.

One oceanic plate subducts under the other, forming a trench and melting into magma far down under the ocean floor. When the magma rises up from this subduction zone, it spills out of vents and cracks in the ocean floor of the overriding plate, where it cools and hardens into volcanic rock and piles up to form a submarine mountain, or **seamount**.

Eventually, over tens of millions of years, these seamounts can get so big that they rise above the surface of the ocean. A chain of volcanic islands can form, strung along the subduction zone like beads on a necklace. This chain is called an **island arc**. It forms a curve, or arc, because it follows the natural curve of the Earth. Island arcs are always found on the landward (continental) side of an ocean trench.

Japan is part of an island arc that formed when the Pacific and North American plates converged. The Philippine islands were created when the Pacific plate collided with the Philippine plate, and the many islands of Indonesia rose as seamounts along the subduction zone of the Australian and Eurasian plates.

DANGER ZONE: THE RING OF FIRE

When all of the volcanoes in the Pacific region are plotted on a map, they form a circle around the Pacific Ocean. This is called the "Ring of Fire," and it includes island nations like Japan and the Philippines, along with parts of Alaska and the western coast of the United States. Half of the world's active volcanoes are located along the Ring of Fire, which marks the boundaries of the large Pacific plate with many other plates. Earthquakes rumble frequently along the Ring of Fire because the Pacific plate boundaries are active and the plate moves relatively fast.

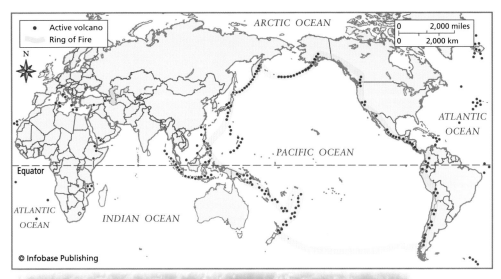

The Ring of Fire, which runs along the border of the Pacific plate, is associated with a large number of active volcanoes. Earthquakes are also more common along the ring.

When an earthquake happens at a trench or plate boundary under the sea, it can trigger a deadly wave called a **tsunami**. This is what happened on December 26, 2004, when a powerful undersea quake triggered a series of deadly tsunamis that killed more than 225,000 people. The earthquake occurred in the Sunda Trench off the western coast of Sumatra, where the India plate (part of the Indo-Australian plate) is subducting under the Burma plate (part of the Eurasian plate). It was the second-largest earthquake ever recorded on a seismograph, measuring 9.1 to 9.3 in magnitude.

Ocean Ridges and Rift Valleys

▲ ▲ ▲

IF ALL THE WATER WERE DRAINED FROM THE ATLANTIC OCEAN, hundreds of mountain peaks would appear. These volcanic mountains, some as tall as 10,000 feet (3,048 m), have never seen the sky. Yet they are part of the longest mountain range in the world: the **Mid-Atlantic Ridge**.

The Mid-Atlantic Ridge was discovered in the 1850s when the U.S. Navy measured the depth of the Atlantic Ocean, all the way across from America to Europe, in preparation for the first intercontinental telegraph line. When scientists completed a map of the ocean floor, they discovered a chain of mountains that ran all the way down the middle of the Atlantic Ocean like a zipper on a coat—from the Arctic Ocean to the southern tip of Africa. Until then, the ocean floor was thought to be relatively flat.

When other ocean floors were mapped, it was discovered that every major ocean in the world has its own underwater mountain chain. There are seven mid-ocean ridges: the Mid-Atlantic Ridge, the Southwest Indian Ridge, the Central Indian Ridge, the Southeast Indian Ridge, the Pacific-Antarctic Ridge, the East Pacific Rise, and the Juan de Fuca Ridge.

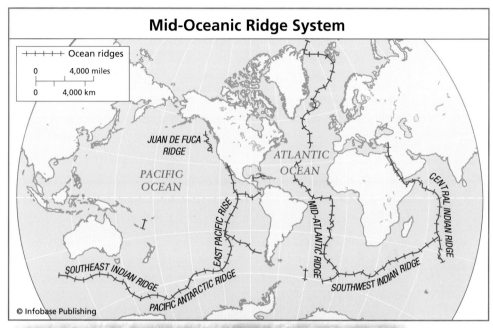

Mid-Oceanic Ridge System

+++++ Ocean ridges

0   4,000 miles

0   4,000 km

JUAN DE FUCA RIDGE

PACIFIC OCEAN

ATLANTIC OCEAN

CENTRAL INDIAN RIDGE

EAST PACIFIC RISE

MID-ATLANTIC RIDGE

SOUTHEAST INDIAN RIDGE

PACIFIC ANTARCTIC RIDGE

SOUTHWEST INDIAN RIDGE

© Infobase Publishing

Mid-ocean ridges mark the undersea boundaries where two plates are diverging, or pulling apart. It is here where new crust is made.

Just as ocean trenches mark the spot where two plates are converging, or coming together, mid-ocean ridges mark the boundaries where plates are diverging, or pulling apart. The Mid-Atlantic Ridge is located where the North American and South American plates are pulling away from the Eurasian and African plates. The Pacific-Antarctic Ridge is the divergent boundary between the Pacific and Antarctic plates. The Southwest Indian Ridge marks the separation of the African and Antarctic plates.

It turns out that all of the ridges are connected, forming one gigantic mid-ocean ridge that runs around the world like the stitching on a baseball, marking the boundaries between tectonic plates. This global ridge is about 40,000 miles (64,000 km) long, and in some places, as much as 3,000 miles (4,800 km) wide.

OCEAN RIFTS: WHERE NEW CRUST IS MADE

So what happens at the mid-ocean ridges? Why are they there? When plates pull apart on the ocean floor, the crust and the underlying lithosphere between them is stretched thin, forming a wide valley known as a **rift zone**. Magma rises up in this "weak spot" through big cracks, or **fissures**, building new volcanic crust and forming underwater mountains—the mid-ocean ridges.

While one side of an oceanic plate is pulling away from another at the rift zone, its other side is sinking down into a deep ocean trench, near the continental coastline. Over tens of millions of years, the rows of mountains formed along the rift zone or mid-ocean ridge move across the ocean floor toward the trenches like lines of marching soldiers. By the time they reach an ocean trench, the mountains have been buried by ocean sediment, and the seafloor is flat.

Like a rolling conveyor belt, the ocean floor moves outward from the rift in both directions and down into the trenches. This cycle is called seafloor spreading (see Chapter 2). Volcanic mountains are formed at both ends of this recycling loop: at the rift zone, where oceanic plates are moving apart; and at the subduction zones, where the oceanic plates are sinking down into the mantle.

About 150 million years ago, the continents of North America, Europe, and Africa were joined together. When the three plates holding these continents began to pull apart, the seafloor between them was stretched, widening the oceans. As the ocean floor spreads, the continents are carried along with it. Today, the continents of North America and Europe are about 3,000 miles (4,800 km) apart. As the Atlantic Ocean floor continues to widen, however, New York City and London are inching a little farther apart each year.

SPEED LIMIT IN THE DIVERGENCE ZONE

Diverging plates move at very different speeds—anywhere from less than 1 inch (2.5 cm) per year to more than 6 inches (15 cm) per year. The plate speed helps determine what a mid-ocean

This computer-generated map of the Atlantic Ocean between North America (*left*) and Europe and Africa (*right*) shows the mid-Atlantic ridge as a light blue curve in the middle of the dark blue ocean floor. The ridge is the longest mountain range in the world, built by magma that rises in the mid-Atlantic rift between diverging plates.

ridge will look like. For example, the rate of spreading along the Mid-Atlantic Ridge averages only about 1 inch (2.5 cm) per year. Slow spreading zones like the Mid-Atlantic Ridge have wide **rift valleys**, up to 12 miles (16.8 km) across, and tall mountains, rising as high as 2 miles (3.2 km) from the ocean floor.

In contrast, the East Pacific Rise just west of South America is a rift zone where the Pacific plate is separating from three others: the Cocos plate, the Nazca plate, and the Antarctic plate. The speed of divergence along the East Pacific Rise is the fastest in the world: The plates are separating at a rate of about 6 inches (15 cm) per year. Because things happen so fast, there is no time for tall mountains to grow along this ridge. Instead, its small peaks are less than 1,000 feet (305 m) in height.

ICELAND: RISING ABOVE THE SEA

There are only a few places in the world where the volcanic mountains of a mid-ocean ridge stick their heads above water. The most famous is the country of Iceland.

Iceland is a big island about the size of Indiana (39,000 square miles or 100,000 square kilometers) that sits right on top of the Mid-Atlantic Ridge. The rift between the North American and Eurasian plates slices right through the middle of the country and is widening at a rate of about 1.3 inches (3.2 cm) per year. Iceland is relatively young: The island rose above the ocean surface along the ridge only about 20 million years ago.

Iceland is a geologist's paradise. Filled with lava flows and hissing steam vents, it is the only place in the world where a divergence zone can be studied on land. More than two dozen volcanoes erupt regularly on Iceland, adding more rock to the island. At Krafla Volcano, cracks in the ground have widened, and new ones appear every few months in what is called the Krafla fissure zone. Lava erupts continuously from these fissures.

Iceland is made up of the main island and many small islands called islets, many of which were formed by volcanic eruptions. Iceland's newest islet was born in 1963. Surtsey, located 20 miles (32 km) south of the big island, peeked its head above water that same year and kept erupting until 1967. The new island is named for Surtur, a giant of fire in Icelandic mythology.

The Azores islands of Portugal also rose above sea level along the Mid-Atlantic Ridge, at the junction between the North American plate and the African and Eurasian plates. The youngest island in the Azores chain is Pico, which rose from the sea about 300,000 years ago.

In 1963, the island of Surtsey rose out of the ocean along the Mid-Atlantic Ridge, making it one of the youngest islands in the world.

AFRICA'S GREAT RIFT VALLEY

When two oceanic plates diverge, a rift with mountain ridges is formed. But what happens on land when two continental plates diverge? In this case, a rift valley is created.

There is no better place to see this in action than East Africa's famous **Great Rift Valley**, where the Earth is literally pulling apart. Up to 60 miles (100 km) wide in some places, the Great Rift Valley runs through eastern Africa for 4,475 miles (7,200 km), from Lake Nyasa in Mozambique north to the Red Sea.

(continued on page 44)

Hot Spots

Volcanic mountain ranges are often found near plate boundaries, where plates are pulling apart or pushing together. But sometimes volcanic activity happens far from any plate boundary—deep within a continent or way out on the ocean floor. These places are called **hot spots.**

Two good examples of hot spots are Yellowstone National Park in Wyoming and the Hawaiian Islands in the Pacific Ocean. Hot spots are isolated places on Earth where the mantle is exceptionally hot and heat rises upward to melt the crust—sort of how a stove burner sets a pot to boiling.

Yellowstone National Park in Wyoming, named for the yellow rock exposed in its **canyon** walls, sits on a giant caldera, a collapsed crater nearly 45 miles (72 km) wide, left by an enormous volcano that erupted 600,000 years ago. The Yellowstone caldera is one of the largest and most active calderas in the world. The same source of underground heat, or **geothermal energy**, that powered the ancient Yellowstone volcano heats more than 10,000 geothermal features in the park today: hot springs, hot pools, bubbling mud pots, and **geysers,** including the famous "Old Faithful," which spouts a column of hot water and steam into the sky every 45 to 110 minutes.

How do hot spots work? Some geologists stick to a theory developed in 1963 by the founder of the hot spot theory, Canadian geophysicist J. Tuzo Wilson. He said that hot spots were long-lasting, exceptionally hot regions below the plates that sent plumes of hot material upward from deep in the mantle. Wilson's research focused on the Hawaiian Islands, noting that the chain of volcanic islands was formed as the Pacific plate moved slowly over a deep, stationary hot spot in the mantle. As one island volcano moves past the hot spot and becomes extinct, another develops over the hot spot, and the cycle is repeated. Over millions of years, a chain of volcanic islands is formed.

The age of each Hawaiian island corresponds with this theory: The oldest island, Kauai, is the farthest from the hot spot. The youngest, Hawaii, with one of the world's most active volcanoes, is over it.

New research shows that the mantle is hotter and more fluid than once thought, leading to a new theory that hot spots are created by stirrings or currents in the upper mantle, caused by the movements of the crustal plates and surface cooling.

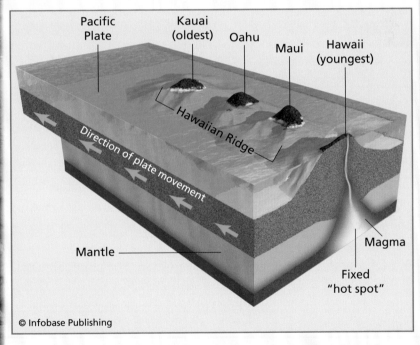

© Infobase Publishing

The Hawaiian island chain was formed by a hot spot—a place where magma rises to the surface far from any plate boundary or rift zone. As the Pacific plate moves slowly over the hot spot, new volcanic islands are formed, one at a time. Hawaii, with the most active volcano in the world, sits over the hot spot today.

(continued from page 41)

The Great Rift Valley splits through the countries of Ethiopia, Kenya, and Tanzania. It is bordered by high volcanic mountains and contains some of the deepest lakes in the world. (Lake Tanganyika is up to 4,823 feet, or 1,470 meters, deep.)

As the crust stretches and thins along this African rift zone, huge cracks called faults form in the Earth, allowing magma to reach the surface. This has created many tall volcanic mountains in East Africa, including the famous snow-capped Mount Kilimanjaro and Mount Kenya. Boiling hot springs also are located throughout the valley.

The African rift begins in the north at the Red Sea, where three plates are diverging in what geologists call a **triple junction**. Here, the Arabian plate (carrying Saudi Arabia and other countries of the Middle East) and two pieces of the African plate—the Nubian and the Somalian—are stretching apart in an area known as the Afar Triangle.

These diverging plates have already pulled Saudi Arabia away from Africa and allowed the Red Sea to flood the valley between them. Geologists believe that, if spreading continues, the three plates at the edge of the African continent will separate completely, allowing the Indian Ocean to flood the area and making the easternmost corner of Africa (the Horn of Africa) a large island.

Of course, none of this will happen soon. The plates are separating today at a speed of about 1 inch (2.5 cm) per year. At this rate, scientists predict the breakup will occur approximately 50 million years from now.

But as anyone who has felt an earthquake knows, plate movement can be unpredictable. The buildup of underground pressure can lead to sudden bursts of movement. In September 2005, hundreds of deep cracks appeared along the African rift zone within a few weeks, and parts of the ground shifted 26 feet (8 m)—almost overnight!

Scientists predict that the Great Rift Valley in Africa, where plates are diverging, will be flooded by the Red Sea millions of years from now. When this happens, a new ocean will form, and the rift will become a mid-ocean range.

5

Fault-block Mountains and Their Valleys

▲▲▲

AT 5:14 A.M. ON APRIL 18, 1906, THE CITY OF SAN FRANCISCO WAS jolted awake by a powerful earthquake. Teacups fell from cupboards. Beds moved across the room. And fires that would burn for nearly five days exploded and merged into one giant inferno, destroying more than 500 city blocks.

When it was all over, as many as 3,000 people were dead. It was one of the worst natural disasters in the history of the United States.

The San Francisco Earthquake was triggered by movement along a 296-mile-long (476 km) section of rock in the San Andreas Fault zone, which stretches for 800 miles (1,287 km) along western California—nearly the entire length of the state. The fault zone marks the boundary where the Pacific and North American plates are sliding past each other.

While the San Francisco quake brought attention to the dangers of living near a fault, it was not until some 50 years later that the relationship of faults to tectonic plates was realized.

WHOSE FAULT WAS IT?

A fault is a large crack, or fissure, that forms when rock under stress breaks suddenly. Once a large crack has formed, it does not repair itself, and the rock on both sides of the crack can move in different directions. If no movement happens, the crack is called a **joint**. If movement occurs, it is called a fault.

Geologists have some special words to describe the rocks along a fault. The **fault plane** is the surface where the two sides of rock meet. It may be vertical or tilted at an angle, known as the **dip**. When the fault plane is dipping and movement has occurred, the uppermost wall is called the **hanging wall,** and the lower wall is the **footwall**. The **fault trace** is the line of the fault as it appears on the Earth's surface. The **strike** is the direction of this line.

Not all faults are visible at the surface; many are located deep underground. Some of the faults along the San Andreas Fault zone are as deep as 10 miles (16 km) underground.

Faults are common along all kinds of plate boundaries because movement of the plates—whether they are grinding past each other, pushing together, or pulling apart—causes rocks to break or fracture. When a giant slab of rock slides up along a fault, a mountain can rise into the sky. When a slab of rock slips down along a fault plane, a valley can form. Faults have shaped mountains and valleys around the world.

TYPES OF FAULTS

There are three basic types of faults: normal, reverse, and strike-slip. A **normal fault** is when one side of rock moves *down* the dipping fault plane. This happens when blocks of rock are being pulled apart, as in a divergence zone. A **reverse fault** is when one side of rock moves *up* the fault plane, sliding over the rock below. This happens when rocks are being pushed together, as in a convergence zone.

Three Types of Faults

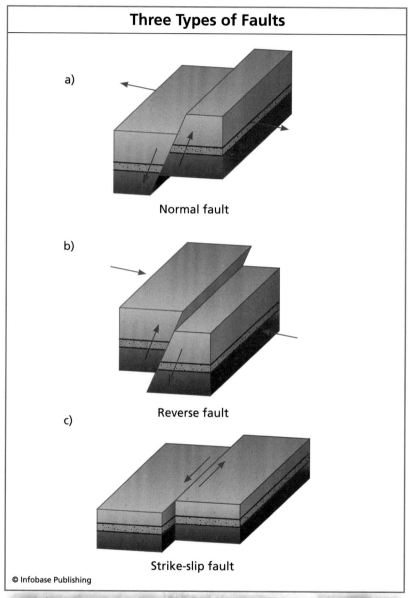

a)

Normal fault

b)

Reverse fault

c)

Strike-slip fault

© Infobase Publishing

Faults, or large cracks in the earth along which movement occurs, help mountains rise up and valleys drop down. Faults are also the cause of earthquakes, which happen when the blocks of rock on each side of a fault move. Normal faults *(a)* are found where the crust is stretching apart. Reverse *(b)* faults are found where the crust is pushing together. A strike-slip fault *(c)* is where two plates are sliding sideways past each other.

A **strike-slip fault** is when two blocks of rock slide sideways past each other along the same horizontal plane. This is the kind of fault that caused the San Francisco Earthquake.

The San Andreas Fault zone lies along the transform plate boundary between the North American plate (sliding slowly southeast) and the Pacific plate (moving northwest). The line or fault trace of the San Andreas Fault is easy to see on land: Fences have broken and roads have shifted along its 800-mile-long (1,287 km) path. Not all faults are visible at the surface. The 1994 Northridge Earthquake was generated by a fault located about 11 miles (18 km) under the city of Los Angeles.

All kinds of faults can cause earthquakes, which happen when rocks along a fault build up pressure, then "slip" suddenly to release that pressure.

NORMAL FAULTS: BUILDING BLOCK MOUNTAINS AND RIFT VALLEYS

Normal faults play an important role in creating rift valleys. Long parallel faults can form on both sides of the widening rift, where plates are diverging. As the valley floor drops *down* between the two faults, steep angled cliffs called **fault scarps** rise up on both sides, forming dramatic fault-block mountains. Some of the fault scarps along Africa's expansive Great Rift Valley rise as high as 6,232 feet (1,900 km) from the valley floor.

Death Valley, in southeastern California, is a rift valley bordered by parallel, normal faults that helped drop the 156-mile-long (251 km) valley as far as 282 feet (86 m) below sea level. As the valley floor lowered, fault-block mountains rose along its borders: the Amargosa Range to the east and the Panamint Range to the west. Thanks to the faults that frame it, Death Valley is the lowest, hottest, driest place in the Western Hemisphere.

When the crust is being slowly pulled apart, a large area can be broken up by dozens of normal faults. As blocks of rock drop down between these normal faults, forming valleys of all sizes, the rocks on each side are lifted up, sometimes forming flat-topped block mountains called **horsts**. This terrain of

The Night the Mountain Broke: Hebgen Lake Quake, 1959

It was just before midnight on August 17, 1959, and the Whitman family was sleeping in their quiet country home in southwestern Montana. Suddenly, Roland Whitman and his wife were awakened by the loud crash of dishes and falling furniture. They ran out of the house, put the children in the car, and started to drive down the dark road toward the nearest town of West Yellowstone, Montana.

Not far from their home, Whitman's wife, Margaret, shouted at her husband to hit the brakes, but it was too late. The car skidded into a 13-foot-deep (4 m) crack in the road, landing headlights-down.

Everyone climbed out. They had fallen into a crack in the earth created minutes earlier by a powerful earthquake.

Just outside of Yellowstone National Park, which sits on the border of Montana and Wyoming, nearly 18,000 campers and park staff had also felt the shock of the powerful quake, which registered 7.5 on the Richter scale. (The San Francisco Earthquake measured 8.3.)

alternating fault-block mountains and rift valleys is called "horst and **graben**."

Horst and graben terrain occurs when fault planes are nearly vertical. When fault planes are dipping, however, the blocks of rock rise at an angle, forming tilted fault-block mountains like those in the **Basin and Range province** of the western United States.

The Sierra Nevada: Tilted to the West

In the long, narrow state of California, there is an inland mountain range that runs parallel to the coastline for 350 miles (560 km).

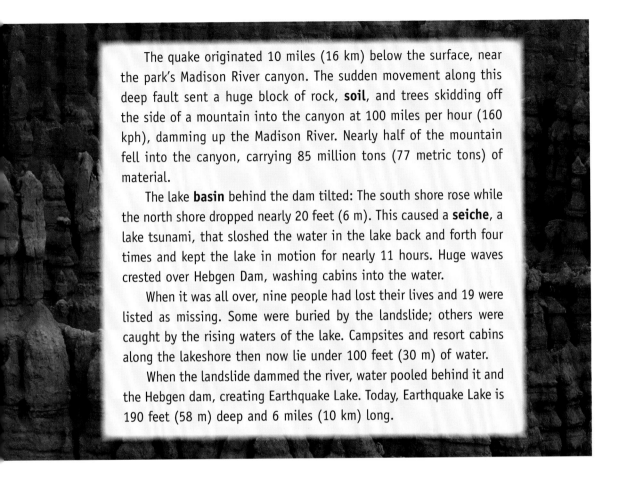

The quake originated 10 miles (16 km) below the surface, near the park's Madison River canyon. The sudden movement along this deep fault sent a huge block of rock, **soil**, and trees skidding off the side of a mountain into the canyon at 100 miles per hour (160 kph), damming up the Madison River. Nearly half of the mountain fell into the canyon, carrying 85 million tons (77 metric tons) of material.

The lake **basin** behind the dam tilted: The south shore rose while the north shore dropped nearly 20 feet (6 m). This caused a **seiche**, a lake tsunami, that sloshed the water in the lake back and forth four times and kept the lake in motion for nearly 11 hours. Huge waves crested over Hebgen Dam, washing cabins into the water.

When it was all over, nine people had lost their lives and 19 were listed as missing. Some were buried by the landslide; others were caught by the rising waters of the lake. Campsites and resort cabins along the lakeshore then now lie under 100 feet (30 m) of water.

When the landslide dammed the river, water pooled behind it and the Hebgen dam, creating Earthquake Lake. Today, Earthquake Lake is 190 feet (58 m) deep and 6 miles (10 km) long.

It is called the Sierra Nevada, which translates from Spanish to "Snowy Range." People who live in crowded, smog-filled Los Angeles like to go to the Sierras (as they are nicknamed) to camp, hike, and ski. The mountains are home to Yosemite National Park and the world's last remaining giant sequoia trees, which can live up to 3,000 years.

The sparkling, gray granite rock of the Sierras is volcanic rock that formed deep underground in a subduction zone more than 150 million years ago. But the Sierras took on their present-day shape more recently. Less than 5 million years ago, the range rose along the eastward-dipping Sierra Nevada frontal fault through a combination of uplift of the block of volcanic

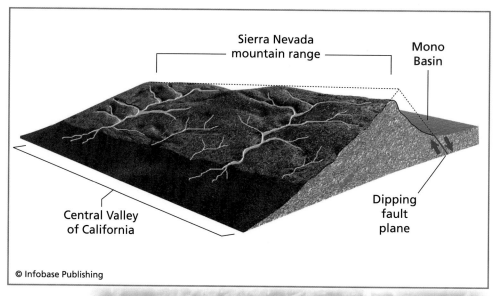

© Infobase Publishing

The Sierra Nevada range in California is a tilted fault-block mountain range. The normal fault that created it is tilted, or dipping. This caused the block of earth on the western side of the fault to rise at a steep angle, forming some of the highest mountains in the United States, while the block on the eastern side dropped down to form a wide valley or basin.

rock on the western side of the fault and sinking of the land on the eastern side.

As a result of this movement along a dipping fault, the Sierra Nevada range has steep scarp mountains on its eastern side and long, gentle slopes on its western side—leading down into California's Central Valley. The Sierras are classic tilted fault-block mountains.

The Tetons: Built on a Fault

The smaller Teton range in Wyoming also rose along a dipping fault plane. Its jagged, snow-covered peaks tower over picturesque Jackson Hole valley, where skiers and cowboys and Hollywood stars work and play. The entire mountain range is part of Grand

Teton National Park, a climbers' paradise and a wildlife haven for bears, wolves, and elk.

Unlike most mountain ranges, the Tetons have no **foot-hills**—lower hills and ridges—that lead up to the higher peaks.

The spectacular Teton mountains in Wyoming rise more than a mile up from the valley floor, known as Jackson Hole (seen in the foreground of this photo). The Tetons began to rise along the dipping Teton fault only about 9 million years ago, making them the youngest range in the Rocky Mountains. Fault zones within the mountains caused the central peaks to rise even higher.

Instead, the mountains rise abruptly 5,000 to 7,000 feet (1,524 to 2,134 m)—almost straight up from the valley floor.

What makes the Tetons look the way they do? It is their fault—that is, the fault that runs along the base of the 40-mile-long (64 km) mountain range like an invisible seam.

The Teton fault is a normal fault that dips eastward and runs parallel to the Teton range. Beginning about 6 million to 9 million years ago, the block on the western side of the fault (the footwall) rose up, while the block on the eastern side of the fault (the hanging wall) slipped down. This movement occurred in fits and starts, each time triggered by a strong earthquake. The Teton fault is still active; earthquakes happen every year. Hikers can hear their deep rumble, but most of the earthquakes are too small to be felt.

Geologists have compared layers of rock on both sides of the Teton fault to see how far each block has moved over time. A layer of rock on top of Mount Moran, at about 12,500 feet (3,810 m), was found on the other side of the fault deep underground, 22,500 feet (6,858 m) below sea level. This means that the Tetons rose an impressive 4.5 inches (11.4 cm) every 100 years.

Fault zones within the mountain range helped the central peaks—the Grand Teton, the Middle Teton, and the Little Teton—rise even higher. Today, the Grand Teton towers over the valley at 13,772 feet (4,198 m).

THRUST FAULTS: WHEN MOUNTAINS MOVE UP AND OVER

Normal faults are common in places where the Earth's crust is pulling apart. They help create rift valleys and block mountains. The opposite of a normal fault is a reverse fault, where a wall of rock moves *up* the fault plane rather than dropping down. Reverse faults are found where rocks are being pushed together—for example, where plates are converging or subducting.

A type of reverse fault frequently found in mountain ranges is the **thrust fault**. Many mountains are formed by thrust faults, which are reverse faults that have shallow, gently dipping fault planes. A slab of rock on one side of the fault slides up and over the other slab of rock. Geologists call the top slab an overthrust. Overthrusts are common in intensely deformed mountain belts, such as the Appalachians and the Himalayas.

The giant slabs of rock that are moved along thrust faults can be many miles long and hundreds to thousands of feet thick. Their movement over time can be dramatic, displacing the rock several miles from its original location and making geologists scratch their heads.

More than 275 million years ago, a continental collision began to form the Appalachian Mountains along the East Coast of the United States. A series of thrust faults pushed mountain-sized blocks, one over the other, in a northwesterly direction. This is known as the Valley and Ridge region.

Pine Mountain in Kentucky is the westernmost thrust block of the Appalachian Mountains. The rocks in the northern portion of Pine Mountain have traveled 4 miles (6.4 km) from their original location. The rocks in the southern part of the mountain (in Tennessee) have migrated 11 miles (18 km).

Considering that the Pine Mountain fault block is thousands of feet thick, it is amazing to think of the force required to move a mountain.

6

Weathering and Erosion

▲▲▲

THE GRAND CANYON IN ARIZONA IS ONE OF THE SEVEN NATURAL wonders of the world. A mile (1.6 km) deep and 20 miles (32 km) wide, the canyon is so enormous it seems impossible to a visitor standing at its rim and looking down. Almost 2 billion years of North American geological history are recorded in its multicolored walls.

Way down at the bottom of the canyon, where the cold, green Colorado River cuts through towering walls of stone, there is a layer of dark gray rock called the Vishnu Schist. It is the oldest exposed rock in the canyon. Geologists have determined that the Vishnu Schist is rock from the roots of the ancient Mazatzal Mountains, which stood on this same piece of the Earth's crust 1.7 billion years ago. Scientific estimates show that the Mazatzals were once as tall as the Himalayas.

What happened to these magnificent peaks of the past? Like most mountains, as soon as they were born, they began to die. Elements of nature—ice, wind, and water—chiseled their peaks, carved their canyons, and slowly but surely brought them down to the ground.

WEATHERING: HOW BIG ROCKS ARE BROKEN INTO BITS

Over hundreds of millions of years, valleys are carved and mountains are worn down by the natural processes of **weathering** and erosion. Weathering happens to rocks where they are. Erosion involves movement: Water, wind, and ice move rocks from one place to another. There are two kinds of weathering: mechanical and chemical.

Mechanical Weathering

Mechanical weathering is when rocks are broken into smaller fragments by nature's elements: ice, water, heat, and pressure. For example, moisture that becomes trapped in joints or cracks in a rock can freeze and make the cracks expand, breaking off chunks of rock. This type of weathering, called **freeze-thaw**, is common in mountains where there are cold temperatures and lots of moisture. Chunks of broken rock collect at the bottom of mountain peaks to form **scree slopes**.

Plants grow in rock cracks, too. As plant roots get bigger and dig in deeper, fragments of rock break off. The heat of a forest fire can also crack rocks open.

Another form of mechanical weathering is **exfoliation**, when thin layers of rock peel off like onion skin over time. This is commonly seen in sedimentary rocks like shale, which breaks apart in flat sheets.

Chemical Weathering

When rocks are exposed to air and water, their chemical structure can change. This is called **chemical weathering**. Rust is a good example of chemical weathering. When a bike or gardening tools are left outside all year, oxygen (air) and water (moisture) convert the metallic iron to its oxidized form: ferric iron, or the orange-brown coating we call rust.

How much a rock will chemically weather depends on the kinds of minerals it contains. Minerals are the building blocks of rocks, sometimes visible as grains of different colors—bits of gold or pink or shiny black. Certain minerals are more susceptible to chemical weathering. Others, called **stable minerals**, retain their chemical structure even when exposed to air and water.

Quartz, the crystal-like mineral often found in granite and sandstone, is a stable mineral. It dissolves very slowly—so slowly that it is sometimes the only mineral left when all others in a rock have weathered away. Most of the sand on Earth is made of tiny, rounded quartz grains. Rocks like granite and sandstone, which contain quartz and other stable minerals, often form the backbones, or ridges, of mountains. How long a mountain will last depends largely on the kind of rock it is made of.

Chemical weathering can make a rock weaker so it crumbles or even dissolves to form something else. For example, when a common rock-forming mineral called feldspar is exposed to water, it partially dissolves to make **clay**.

Climate affects the amount of weathering that occurs. Limestone, made of the accumulated skeletons of tiny marine creatures on the seafloor, dissolves more easily in rainwater than other kinds of rock. To see how limestone stands up to the weather, one need only visit an old cemetery.

Headstones from the 1700s and early 1800s are mostly made of white limestone. Many are cracked or worn smooth so the names and dates are difficult to read. More recent headstones are made of gray or pink granite. The words on the granite headstones are as crisp and clear as the day they were chiseled. This is because granite contains stable minerals like quartz and biotite.

In the dry desert, limestone has a longer life. Without moisture to eat away at it, chemical weathering happens very slowly, if at all. This is one reason why the nearly 5,000-year-old pyramids of Egypt, thought to be built of giant limestone blocks, still stand today.

EROSION: MOVING ROCKS AND MAKING DIRT

Weathering crumbles rocks into smaller pieces that can be carried away by gravity, water, wind, and ice. This movement of rock materials is called erosion.

Mount Rushmore:
Presidents Carved in Rock

It is hard not to be amazed by the story of Mount Rushmore National Memorial in South Dakota. It took 14 years, from 1927 to 1941, to complete the carving of four presidents' faces on the top of a mountain. More than 400 workers helped sculptor Gutzon Borglum bring his vision to life with dynamite, drills, and chisels.

(continues)

Mount Rushmore was chiseled over the course of 14 years. The large pile of rocks cascading down from the monument is the granite that was chipped away while the faces were being carved.

(continued)

When they were done, George Washington, Thomas Jefferson, Theodore Roosevelt, and Abraham Lincoln stood together, gazing out from the mountain as if they were hiding there all along, just waiting for someone to chisel them out.

Each face is approximately 60 feet (18 m) high, as tall as a six-story building. Their features are amazingly realistic: Strands of hair, eyeballs, and even Lincoln's famous mole are depicted.

Borglum chose Mount Rushmore partly because of its rock. Part of the Black Hills region, the mountain is mostly made of fine-grained granite, formed deep underground 1.6 billion years ago and brought to the surface through uplift and erosion of the more fragile sedimentary rocks above it. Granite stands up well to erosive forces like wind, rain, snow, and frost. The granite found in the Black Hills, called Harney Peak granite, is very resistant, eroding only 1 inch (2.5 cm) every 10,000 years.

To slow the erosion even more, Borglum had workers fill in all the cracks in the faces with a mixture of white lead, linseed oil, and granite dust. Filling the cracks would prevent freeze-thaw weathering. In 1991, the National Park Service found an even better material for filling cracks: a silicone, or plastic, sealant. Every fall, maintenance workers dangle from ropes in harnesses to inspect the faces for cracks.

All of this may help Borglum's wish come true: that the presidents memorialized at Mount Rushmore will "endure until the wind and rain alone shall wear them away."

Erosion can change the landscape even more than an earthquake, though the changes happen very slowly. Streams and rivers carry rocks, pebbles, and sand downstream, grinding them into smooth particles like a rock-tumbling machine and digging out canyons and valleys along the way. Glaciers, giant frozen rivers of slow-moving ice, scrape and carve the Earth as they lift and carry chunks of rock as big as cars. Waves crash into rocks and tumble them into sand grains. Fierce desert winds carve into soft rock like sculptors wielding sandblasters. Sand dunes are formed when wind pushes the sand into giant piles.

Working together, the forces of weathering and erosion turn boulders into rocks, rocks into pebbles, and pebbles into sand. Gravity brings all these bits and pieces of rock tumbling down mountains and hills into valleys, where they accumulate on the ground and in rivers as sediment. Mixed with the organic remains of plants and animals, sediment forms soil and com-presses and hardens into layers over time to make sedimentary rocks.

How quickly does erosion happen? It depends on the local climate, the type of rock, and the steepness of the landscape. Generally, erosion happens faster in wetter climates and in higher places, where gravity and melting snow send more rocks tumbling downhill. Sometimes erosion happens very fast, without warning. A **landslide** can happen when an entire mountain slope suddenly gives way to gravity or torrential rain. This can be disastrous for anything in its path.

Stream Erosion: Carving Out Canyons and Valleys

Every spring, the snow up high in the Green Mountains of Vermont begins to melt. At first, the icy water, or snowmelt, trick-les down the mountainside in streams and little waterfalls. But as the air temperature gets hotter, the snow melts faster, and soon the water is gushing downhill, signaling the start of what locals call the "mud season."

As the water flows, it digs little **gullies** into the sides of mountains. Over millions of years, these gullies get deeper and wider, eventually forming steep-walled canyons. Animals and hikers travel up and down mountains through these canyons.

The Grand Canyon of the Yellowstone is still being carved by the Yellowstone River. The steep sides and V-shape of this canyon indicate that it is a river-carved canyon; canyons carved by glaciers are U-shaped.

When a stream heads downhill, it sweeps up rocks and pebbles along the way. It may join up with other streams and form a river. Through the abrasive action of the stones and sediments it carries along the bottom, a river digs out a **V-shaped valley**. Geologists know that V-shaped valleys are formed by streams and rivers, while **U-shaped valleys** are carved out by glaciers.

THE LIFE CYCLE OF A RIVER VALLEY

A valley is a broad area of low-lying land located between hills or mountains, often with a river or stream flowing through it. Valleys can be small, like the little gullies in a farmer's field, or they can be huge, like the Grand Canyon. (A canyon is just a deep valley cut by a stream or river.)

Valleys eroded by water are different from rift valleys created by plate tectonics. Rift valleys may also have rivers, but they have parallel faults and block mountains at their borders (see Chapter 5).

Young river valleys are steeper and narrower than older valleys. This is because of the life cycle of a river. A young river flows rapidly downhill in a fairly straight line, carving out a narrow, V-shaped valley. Hard rock in its path may resist erosion, causing rapids and waterfalls to form as the water forces its way around these obstacles.

As time goes by, the steep sides of the valley are worn down by weathering and begin to slope gently toward the river. Now the river **meanders**, cutting side to side like a snake and creating winding, S-shaped loops.

Every time the river floods its banks, usually in the spring when the snow melts, more and more sediment is deposited along the sides of the river in what is called the **floodplain**. Older valleys are wide and flat, with smooth floodplains bordering their rivers.

UPLIFT AND THE GRAND CANYON: NEW LIFE FOR AN OLD RIVER

If enough sediment or ice is deposited in one large area, the crust can sink from the extra weight, forming a bowl-shaped depression called a basin. But just as the crust can sink, it can also rise when large amounts of rock are removed by erosion or when something forces it up from below. This rebounding of the crust is called **uplift**.

An old river can be reborn when the land over which it flows is uplifted. The change in elevation makes the river flow faster, and it starts cutting down again, making the valley deeper and steeper. This is how the Grand Canyon was made.

Niagara Falls: Eroding Away

Niagara Falls, the popular tourist destination located at the border of Canada and New York on the Niagara River, has been in existence for more than 10,000 years. But it has not always been where it is, surrounded by glittering hotels and souvenir shops.

Ten thousand years ago, the falls were located 7 miles (11 km) north of their present location. In another 10,000 years, they will be somewhere else.

Like most waterfalls, Niagara Falls is **receding**. This means it is slowly moving upriver, back toward the source from which its water flows. Water always flows downhill, and the Niagara River flows north from Lake Erie, located at 578.5 feet (176 m) above sea level, to Lake Ontario, at 246 feet (75 m) above sea level.

The waterfall is moving back because of erosion. The rock at the top of Horseshoe Falls, the bigger of the two Niagara waterfalls, is made of tough dolomite. But even dolomite is broken by the thundering water that pours over the cliff at almost 70 miles an hour (113 kph). When a break occurs, a notch is formed, and the whole cliff begins to move backward as the churning water erodes the softer rocks below. This cycle repeats itself again and again.

Until the early 1950s, the Horseshoe Falls eroded at an average rate of 3 feet (1 m) per year. But electric companies, which use the power of the Niagara River to generate **hydroelectric power**, have diverted or funneled off large amounts of water above the falls, which has reduced the water flow and slowed the rate of erosion to only 1 foot (30 cm) per year.

Over centuries of flooding and depositing sediment along its banks, a river may create a broad, flat floodplain, such as Iceberg Canyon in Arizona.

The Grand Canyon is one of the most dramatic examples of river erosion in the world. It was carved by the mighty Colorado River, which came into being in the Rocky Mountains some 60 million to 70 million years ago. The source of the Colorado River, or its **headwaters** (sometimes a lake or a glacier), is located high in the mountains.

About 6 million years ago, the Colorado **Plateau**—a large platform of land at the foot of the Rocky Mountains—was uplifted over half a mile (1 km) higher than the land to its west. This made the Colorado River surge into youthful action, cutting down hard and fast into the layers of rock that would become the walls of the Grand Canyon.

DOME MOUNTAINS: UNCOVERED BY EROSION

Uplift can happen in lots of different ways. The crust can rebound slowly when a heavy load is lifted, or it can be pushed up gradually from below by the pressure of rising magma. Dome mountains are made by magma that is trapped underground and pushes the rock up into a bubble-like dome.

The Black Hills in South Dakota are dome mountains. Despite their name, the Black Hills are really mountains that feature the highest point in the state: Harney Peak, at 7,242 feet (2,207 m). The Black Hills range is 125 miles (201 km) long and 65 miles (105 km) wide.

Uplift and erosion work together to form dome mountains. The core of the Black Hills is granite that formed deep underground when magma gradually rose, cooled, and hardened, pushing the overlying sedimentary rocks up into dome shapes. About 70 million years ago, the whole Black Hills region began to uplift, bringing these domes of granite closer to the surface. Erosion removed the overlying layers of soft shales and marine sedimentary rocks, revealing the granite domes beneath. In all, more than 6,000 feet (1,829 m) of sedimentary rock layers were removed by erosion from the central part of the Black Hills.

7

The Power of Ice

▲ ▲ ▲

EVERYONE KNOWS THE TERRIFYING TALE OF THE *TITANIC*, THE DOOMED ship that sank in 1912 when it hit an **iceberg** in the middle of the night, killing more than 1,500 people. The broken ship was found on the bottom of the cold North Atlantic 73 years later.

But what about the iceberg? Where did it come from, and where did it go?

No one knows for sure, though photographs were taken of a few suspect icebergs in the area shortly after the accident. One even had a stripe of red paint along its bottom edge, indicating that a ship may have recently collided with it.

The problem is that there are nearly 200 icebergs floating in the North Atlantic during the cold winter months. These moving islands of ice have broken off, or **calved**, from a **glacier** or **ice sheet** and can float for a couple of months before melting away.

Most of the icebergs in the North Atlantic come from Greenland, a huge, ice-covered island that is considered the northernmost land on Earth. Greenland has hundreds of glaciers.

WHAT IS A GLACIER?

Glaciers are thick masses of ice created by snow that has packed down hard, changed its crystal structure to ice, and started to "flow" under the pressure of its own weight. There are three layers in a glacier: The top layer is snow; the middle layer, called **névé**, is a mixture of snow and ice; and the bottom layer is pure

International Ice Patrol

The *Titanic*'s fatal collision with an iceberg in 1912 made the world worry about the dangers of travel in the North Atlantic, where Greenland's glaciers send hundreds of icebergs drifting south each year.

In the aftermath of the disaster, the U.S. Navy assigned two cruisers to watch for icebergs in the area where the *Titanic* sank. In 1913, the first International Conference on the Safety of Life at Sea determined that the United States should manage an official iceberg patrol service.

Today, the U.S. Coast Guard's International Ice Patrol (IIP) is funded by 17 countries. During ice season, usually February through July, the IIP uses airplane radar surveys and information radioed in from ships to pinpoint icebergs, predict their future paths, and produce an "Ice Bulletin" so ships know how far south they should go to avoid the danger zone.

Most of the icebergs that calve off Greenland drift south in the Labrador Current to the Grand Banks off the coast of Newfoundland. The Grand Banks, where the *Titanic* sank, is an important fishing area and a pathway for ships traveling between North America and Europe. It is also where the frigid Labrador Current meets the warm Gulf Stream—a temperature clash that produces thick fog, making it almost impossible to see icebergs.

ice. Glaciers form at high elevations (usually on mountains) and usually closer to the Earth's poles—wherever there is snow that does not melt away in the summer.

Glaciers are found on all of the world's continents except Australia. There are even glaciers in Africa. More than two-thirds of the Earth's freshwater exists as ice in the form of glaciers and

Since it was established, the IIP has prevented any loss of life due to a ship's collision with an iceberg. It also plays an important role in honoring the victims of the *Titanic*. Every year on April 15, the anniversary of the tragedy, a plane flies low and crew members drop flowers from the open cargo door into the cold, dark waters of the North Atlantic.

When glaciers drop pieces of ice into the ocean, it is called "calving." Hubbard Glacier in Alaska has a 6-mile (10 km) border with the ocean, where many tourists come to watch the dramatic calving.

ice sheets. When glaciers melt, the water goes into mountain streams, which flow into rivers and lakes, providing drinking water and hydroelectric power for people. The city of Tacoma, Washington, gets its electricity from a river that is fed by the Nisqually Glacier.

Icebergs and some glaciers are known for their striking blue color. The reason for this is complicated, but it has to do with how sunlight is absorbed by ice. As ice compresses, the tiny air bubbles that make it look white disappear. Dense glacial ice can absorb all of the colors of the rainbow except blue. So blue is what we see.

HOW DO GLACIERS MOVE?

As dangerous as a chunk of ice is to a ship at sea, it can do a lot of damage on land, too. In fact, the hard ice and chunks of stone in glaciers erode the landscape even more than rivers do, scraping mountain peaks and scouring out valleys as they grind along.

Glaciers move by sliding slowly downhill on a thin layer of water or by spreading out slowly from the inside. If you push down on pizza dough, it spreads out. Pressure (from your hand) makes the dough spread. Glaciers work in a similar way. The pressure from the overlying ice makes the "inner" ice spread out, and gravity naturally makes it move downhill or outward from a central point. The whole thing slides over rock on a thin layer of water, which comes from the melting ice or water that has seeped through cracks. Spreading and sliding may happen together or independently.

A glacier's movement depends on the amount of ice, the steepness of its environment, and the pull of gravity. As a glacier slowly advances down a mountain, it picks up rocks, gravel, trees, and even bus-sized boulders along the way. All of these materials become part of the glacier, like ingredients stirred into a thick soup. As the glacier churns along, the ingredients are broken up into smaller and smaller pieces. This process of glacial erosion is similar to the way a river helps rocks disintegrate. Like rivers,

Valley glaciers move slowly down mountains, pushing rocks and trees out of their way. When they retreat, or melt back upward, they leave characteristic U-shaped valleys that allow geologists to trace their paths. Smaller valley glaciers can feed into one large glacier, just as smaller streams feed into a river.

glaciers grind rocks into smaller and smaller bits, so small that they become **rock flour**. This glacial deposit can end up in rivers, lakes, and oceans.

Glaciers move at a wide range of speeds, anywhere from 1 inch (2.5 cm) to 150 feet (46 m) a day. The Lambert-Fisher Glacier in Antarctica is a speed demon, moving half a mile (0.8 km) each year. Glaciers can speed up or slow down over time. When a glacier suddenly picks up its pace, it is called a **surge**.

In 1953, the Kutiah Glacier in Pakistan broke the record for the fastest glacial surge. It moved more than 7.5 miles (12 km) in three months, averaging about 370 feet (112 m) per day.

As a glacier moves over uneven ground, deep cracks can form in the ice, similar to the way faults form in rock. These cracks, called **crevasses**, are extremely dangerous for mountain climbers, who must lay ladders across a crevasse, then tiptoe to the other side in their heavy mountaineering boots. Many have accidentally stumbled into crevasses up to 100 feet (30 m) deep. Some are successfully rescued; others are lost forever in the icy depths of a glacier.

VALLEY GLACIERS

There are two basic types of glaciers: **valley glaciers** and **continental glaciers**. Valley glaciers flow down mountains. From below, a valley glacier looks like a giant frozen tongue stretching down the mountain. The forward part of the glacier (the tip of the tongue) is called the **snout**. It pushes rocks and other debris out of its way, sucking some up and carrying them along.

Mountain valleys are transformed by glaciers. V-shaped river valleys are scooped out to become U-shaped glacial valleys. They are wider, rounder, and flatter on the bottom than river valleys. This is because glaciers scour the bottom and sides of a valley, while rivers cut straight down.

When a valley glacier moves down a mountain, it carves out distinctive features. Some of the world's most famous mountain peaks were sculpted by glaciers. A **cirque** is a large bowl formed at the head of a glacier by scouring ice. When the ice melts away, a small lake may form in this bowl. An **arête** (the French word for "fish bone") is a knifelike ridge that has been carved by cirques meeting back-to-back on either side of a mountain. A **horn** is a mountain peak that has been deeply sculpted on several sides by glaciers. One of the most famous is the Matterhorn, a classic peak in the Swiss Alps.

Tributary glaciers flow down the smaller canyons and valleys of surrounding mountains, merging into the main valley glacier. This is similar to the way mountain streams merge to form a bigger river. When the main glacier begins to melt and retreat, the tributary valleys are left at a higher elevation than the main valley. Now they are called **hanging valleys**. Spectacular waterfalls spill from hanging valleys, plunging to the big valley below. Bridal Veil Falls, which flows from a hanging valley, is one of the most picturesque spots in California's Yosemite National Park, much of which was carved by glaciers.

Lauterbrunnen Valley in Switzerland was carved out long ago by a huge glacier that left nearly vertical walls in its path. Waterfalls spill down from hanging valleys where smaller, tributary glaciers once fed into the huge, incredibly thick glacier.

Valley glaciers begin high up on the mountain, flowing slowly out of **ice fields** that span several peaks or even an entire mountain range. A valley glacier can travel a long way. Like rivers, valley glaciers flow with gravity toward the sea. The Bering Glacier in Alaska is 118 miles (190 km) long, stretching from the St. Elias Mountains to the Gulf of Alaska.

When a glacier spills into the sea, it is called a **tidewater glacier**. Icebergs break off of these glaciers, like big boats launching from a frozen dock. When a tidewater glacier retreats, it leaves behind a deep U-shaped valley. This valley can be flooded with seawater, creating a **fjord**. A boat cruise in a fjord offers travelers spectacular mountain scenery, with steep walls rising on both sides of the flooded glacial valley.

One of the best-documented retreats of a glacier was in Alaska's Glacier Bay. Today, cruise ships take people to see icebergs and glaciers up close in the bay. But only a couple of hundred years ago, this would not have been possible. In 1794, explorer Captain George Vancouver found a huge glacier where Glacier Bay is now. It was 20 miles (32 km) wide, more than 4,000 feet (1,219 m) thick, and stretched more than 100 miles (160 km) from its source in the St. Elias Mountains. By 1879, when naturalist John Muir went to the same spot, the glacier had retreated 48 miles (77 km) back toward the mountains, and a bay had formed.

Today, in Glacier Bay National Park, up to a dozen tidewater glaciers calve into the bay. Lucky visitors can witness the birth of an iceberg, when a gigantic block of ice breaks off and crashes into the water.

GLACIERS ADVANCE AND RETREAT

Glaciers advance down a mountain as they grow, and they recede, or pull back, as they melt. If the rate of snow accumulation is higher than the rate of melting, the glacier will advance. If the opposite is true, the glacier will retreat. A glacier can advance and retreat many times throughout its history, depending on how the climate changes.

As it advances, a glacier scrapes away rock and soil, picking it up and pushing it ahead, then depositing it at its snout. All of the material deposited by glaciers is called **drift**. When glacial drift forms a ridge in the land, marking the point where a glacier began to melt or retreat, it is called **till**. These ridges made of glacial till are called **moraines**. Glacial till makes fertile

Glacier National Park: Melting Away?

If you want to see a glacier in the United States, there would seem no better place to go than Glacier National Park in Montana. But you had better go soon. By 2030, scientists predict that all of the park's glaciers will be gone.

In 1850, there were 150 glaciers in the area of Glacier National Park. Today, there are only 27 glaciers, and all of them are shrinking, or receding. Most of the remaining glaciers are small compared to their original size.

To understand why and how the glaciers are shrinking, scientists with the U.S. Geological Survey are focusing their research on seven glaciers in one section of the park. One of them, Sperry Glacier, is a benchmark glacier, which means that data is collected on it annually. Since 1913, Sperry Glacier has lost about one-third of its ice. Grinnell Glacier has shrunk in size by more than 40% in the last 30 years.

Photographs are taken of all of the glaciers every five years. Aerial photography and satellite images are also used. Luckily, the Glacier Park archives contain about 12,000 photographs taken in the park since the late 1800s, so direct comparisons can be made.

The glaciers are getting less snow in the winter and melting earlier in the spring. Scientists blame slowly rising global temperatures for what is happening to the glaciers in the park and elsewhere in the world.

farmland. Many forests and meadows and farms sit on ancient moraines. By looking at moraines and other signs of glacial movement such as scratches or **striations** in the rock, geologists can trace the path of a glacier that melted long ago.

CONTINENTAL GLACIERS: BLANKETS OF ICE

Continental glaciers are massive **ice sheets** that cover an area of more than 19,300 square miles (50,000 square km). As recently as 18,000 years ago, continental glaciers covered all of Canada and some of the northern United States, northern Europe, and Asia. This most recent **ice age** happened during the Pleistocene epoch, between 2 million and 10,000 years ago. (We are living in the Holocene epoch, which started 10,000 years ago.)

An ice age is a cooler period of the Earth's history when glaciers advance, sometimes covering large areas of land with ice sheets or continental glaciers. There have been several ice ages in the last 800 million years.

We are not in an ice age now. Only Greenland and Antarctica are covered by ice sheets. More than 98% of the world's ice is found in these two countries. More than 80% of Greenland is covered with ice that is, on average, 1.7 miles (2.8 km) thick. The ice sheet on Antarctica is at least 40 million years old and more than 13,780 feet (4,200 m) thick in some places. Huge mountains are buried under Antarctica's ice, but only some—the Transantarctic Mountains—rise above the snow.

Ice shelves form along the coastlines of ice sheets. An ice shelf is a seaward extension of the ice sheet, floating on the ocean yet still attached to the mainland. Ice shelves surround most of the Antarctic continent.

Ice caps are miniature ice sheets, found mostly in polar regions. The volcanic island of Iceland has several ice caps. The largest is Vanajökull, measuring 3,150 square miles (8,160 square km) in size and up to 3,280 feet (1,000 m) thick. Ironically, the Vanajökull Glacier covers up a number of large volcanoes.

REBOUND: WHEN THE WEIGHT IS LIFTED

Glacial ice is thick and dense, which makes it extremely heavy. The land beneath parts of the West Antarctic Ice Sheet may be compressed up to 1.5 miles (2.5 km) below sea level, due to the tremendous weight of the ice. The crust in central Greenland is also compressed to below sea level.

When continental glaciers retreat, the land breathes a sigh of relief, slowly rebounding upward. This is happening today in Scandinavia and the British Isles, which were covered by ice until about 11,000 years ago, when the last ice age ended. Sweden has risen 656 feet (200 m) since then and is still rising about an inch (2.5 cm) per year.

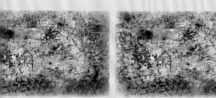

8

Mapping
the Future

▲ ▲ ▲

WHEN BRADFORD WASHBURN MADE THE FIRST MAP OF ALASKA'S
Mount McKinley, the tallest peak in North America, he did it the
old-fashioned way. He climbed the mountain several times and
took pictures of it from the air, hanging out of the open door of
a small airplane.

Washburn was a mountaineer and cartographer, or mapmaker, who photographed and mapped some of the world's highest peaks and one of its most famous valleys, Arizona's Grand
Canyon. Before he died in 2007 at the age of 96, Washburn had
created 24 maps, completed the first ascents of seven North
American peaks, and helped to revise the official height of Mount
Everest.

The kinds of maps Washburn made were **topographic maps**.
Unlike road maps, which present a two-dimensional view, topographic maps offer a three-dimensional view of the land, showing changes in elevation. A topographic map is like an aerial
view of the ground, with **contour lines** outlining the shapes of
mountains, valleys, lakes, and other geologic features.

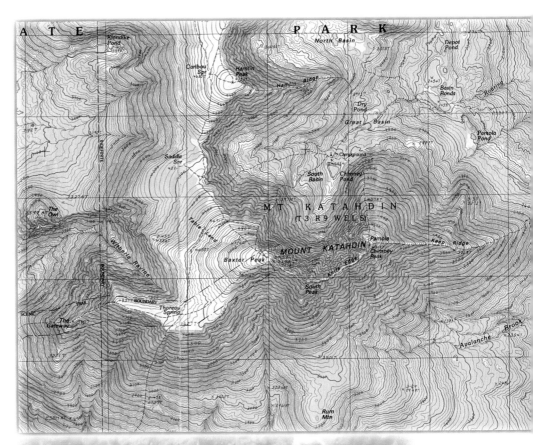

A topographic map uses contour lines to depict elevational changes in an area. All points along a line are at the same elevation. When the lines are closer together, as around Mount Katahdin on the map above, the ground is steeper. When the lines are farther apart, the land is more level—as in a valley.

Topographic maps are used by geologists, biologists, hikers, skiers, airplane pilots, engineers—anyone who needs to know the layout of the land in wild places. On a typical topographic map made by the U.S. Geological Survey, each contour line represents a 100-foot (30 m) change in elevation. Where the lines are closer together, the ground is steeper; where they are farther apart, the ground is flatter. Heavily forested areas are colored green. Rivers and lakes are marked in blue. Triangles mark the summits of mountains.

THE VIEW FROM SPACE: SATELLITE IMAGES

Washburn made most of his topographic maps by hand from aerial photographs. But in the 1970s, the first satellite photographs of Earth became available through NASA's Earth Resources Technology Satellite (later renamed Landsat 1).

Satellite photographs are digital, which means they can be stored, shared, and enhanced on a computer. Now, instead of looking at contour maps, we can *see* the shape and texture of large areas, including entire mountain chains. Scientists can access these images and manipulate them to get a clearer view of landscape features like mountains, valleys, glaciers, and rivers.

In 2007, an international team of scientists pieced together more than 1,000 satellite images to produce the most geologically accurate, true-color photographic map of Antarctica. (Older maps of the continent were made with aerial photographs and data collected by survey ships.) The new map will help scientists plan expeditions, monitor ice flows, and determine the kinds of rocks that make up Antarctica.

NASA operates more than a dozen Earth-Observing Satellites (EOS) equipped with a variety of scientific instruments that are monitoring changes in the land, ocean, and atmosphere. Anyone can view the latest satellite images on NASA's Earth Observatory Web site. Google Earth has also created interactive, 3-D maps that combine satellite and aerial photographs so that anyone with a computer can access detailed images of the Earth.

THE SPACE SHUTTLE: RADAR TOPOGRAPHY

Satellite photographs are beautifully detailed when the sky is clear and nothing obscures the view. But a different kind of image is useful for creating topographic maps of places that are hidden by clouds or in the dark canyons of mountains.

Topographic maps are being replaced or enhanced by images taken from space. This 3-D image of the Teton mountain range was created by combining elevation data from the USGS and the space shuttle's radar topographic mission with photographs taken by the Landsat 7 satellite. This image makes it easy to visualize the fault line along which the Grand Teton mountains rose and the Jackson Hole Valley (*foreground*) lowered.

In 2000, the space shuttle Endeavour carried a special radar instrument aboard to gather data over 80% of the Earth's surface. Unlike cameras, radars operate day and night and can penetrate cloud cover because they work by bouncing radio waves off the Earth. That data can then be used to create a 3-D image of the Earth's surface. The goal of the 11-day Shuttle Radar Topography

Mission was to produce the most accurate and complete topographic map of the Earth ever assembled.

Scientists are using radar images from the shuttle mission to study geologic features in remote places around the world. For example, geologists from Cornell University are combining radar images of the Andes mountains with satellite images to look closely at areas that have never been mapped due to heavy cloud cover. They hope to learn more about how the Andes were formed. Their research may help scientists prepare better for earthquakes in the active Andes subduction zone. It may also provide a more accurate picture of the sources of the Amazon River, a vital water resource for much of South America.

GEOLOGIC MAPS: THE FIELD WORK OF GEOLOGISTS

A topographic map allows scientists to see the shape of the Earth's surface, but a **geologic map** reveals what it is made of. Geologic maps look like abstract paintings, with blocks of multihued colors indicating rock types and ages, and bold lines marking faults and folds.

A geologic map begins with aerial or satellite photos, but the rest of the mapmaking work takes place in the field. Geologists must hike into mountains and valleys to collect rock and soil samples and observe the direction of features such as faults and folds. They might also drill into the Earth with a hollow pipe to pull up a core sample showing the different layers of sediment below.

Just as it takes training to speak a foreign language, it takes special knowledge to read a geologic map. Symbols and colors define rock type, age, anticlines and synclines, the strike and dip of faults, and water sources. Some maps also show a cross section, or underground view, of the area that was mapped.

Geologic maps are not just for geologists. They are important tools for engineers and scientists who build roads and other structures, and those who work with fossil fuels (oil, coal, and natural gas), minerals (such as gold), and underground water supplies (groundwater). They can also help scientists predict when and where an earthquake or landslide might occur.

The first complete geologic map of Mount Everest was published by Oxford University in 2003. Oxford University geologist Mike Searle climbed the mountain six times over 22 years, collecting hundreds of rock samples and analyzing them in his lab to connect them with information from satellite and aerial photographs. His research showed that the force of the collision between India and Asia was more powerful than anyone had realized.

GIS: PUTTING IT ALL TOGETHER

In the past, geologists used compasses to identify their location in the field; today, they use the **Global Positioning System (GPS)**. A portable GPS device communicates with 24 well-spaced satellites orbiting 12,500 miles (20,000 km) above the Earth's surface. With a GPS instrument, a scientist can determine his or her geographical position on Earth to within a few feet, even in the most rugged and inaccessible terrain.

The accuracy of GPS in collecting field data, combined with advances in satellite and radar imagery, has led to a new computer technology called **Geographic Information Systems (GIS)**. GIS allows users to combine digital data from different sources and "layer" them together to create a single map or image that tells a story about the relationship of elements in a particular place. A GIS map could show the distribution of grizzly bears, glaciers, and huckleberry plants in Glacier National Park, all plotted with symbols on a satellite map.

GIS maps give scientists a visual tool to explain complicated environmental issues to policy makers and the public. One of those issues is the fragile health of mountain ecosystems.

THE FUTURE FOR MOUNTAINS

Mountains are found throughout the world, from Antarctica to Alaska. They cover one-fourth of the land and provide a home for one-tenth of the world's population and some of its rarest plants and animals. Mountains represent some of the last truly wild places on Earth, where people can enjoy and explore nature. Perhaps most importantly, half of the world's population depends on freshwater that flows into streams and rivers from melting snow and ice high in the mountains.

Mountains look indestructible, but they contain fragile ecosystems that are vulnerable to human activities and climate change. Humans are speeding up erosion in mountainous areas by cutting down forests, building roads, stripping the land for farming, and tearing into mountain slopes to get minerals and coal. These erosive activities can pollute the water supply.

Climate change—in this case the warming of global temperatures—is speeding up the melting of glaciers, causing damaging floods and changing the growth cycles of plants.

Mountains offer many benefits to humans: water resources, forest products, a refuge for threatened species, and unspoiled recreation areas. But they can also pose hidden dangers. Because mountainous areas are filled with faults and often located near plate boundaries, they are often the site of devastating natural disasters such as earthquakes, floods, landslides, **avalanches**, and volcanic eruptions.

To monitor the changes and potential dangers in mountain ecosystems, and to predict what will happen in the future, it is important to create baseline maps of all the world's mountains, including their glaciers, rock types, water resources, and plants and animals. Thanks to satellite technology, geologists are better equipped than ever to do this.

Working together as a global community, geologists can help decrease the impact of natural disasters, monitor and predict the effects of climate change, and increase our ability to conserve and protect the world's most valuable natural resources. They also hope to learn more about how mountains and valleys were formed hundreds of millions of years ago, before humans became part of the picture.

Glossary

▲

Altitude   The height of a mountain, from sea level to its highest point.

Anticline   A rock fold that arches upward (convex); the opposite of syncline.

Arête   The jagged ridge at the top of a cirque.

Asthenosphere   The hot, partly molten layer of the Earth below the lithosphere, found in the upper mantle.

Avalanche   The event that occurs when a large mass of material—snow, ice, soil, or rock—falls or slides rapidly downhill under the force of gravity.

Basalt   A dark, fine-grained igneous (volcanic) rock that forms much of the oceanic crust.

Basin   A very large circular or elliptical depression in the land.

Basin and Range province   An area in the western United States that features a series of alternating valleys (basins) and mountains (ranges).

Caldera   A basin-shaped volcanic depression at least 1 mile (1.6 km) in diameter that typically forms after a volcano erupts.

Calve   The action of releasing an iceberg or a mass of ice (as from a glacier).

Canyon   A large, deep valley with steep sides, often formed by stream erosion.

Chain   A connected series of mountains or mountain ranges.

Chemical weathering   The breakdown of surface rock due to chemical reactions mostly involving water and air (oxygen).

Cirque   A steep, bowl-shaped depression high on a mountain that is formed at the head of a glacier and often has a small lake or pond at its base.

Clay   A fine-grained soil that can be shaped when wet and is produced by the chemical decomposition of rocks.

Continental drift   The theory that the continents have moved their relative positions over time, due to movement and interactions of the Earth's tectonic plates.

Continental glacier   A thick, continuous glacier covering more than 19,300 square miles (50,000 square km) and moving independently.

Contour lines   Lines on a map, showing topography of the land's changing elevation. All points along a single contour line have the same elevation.

Convergent boundary   The boundary between two tectonic plates that are moving toward each other. Mountains, volcanoes, and trenches are formed along convergent boundaries.

Core   The centermost part of the Earth, probably made of iron and nickel, consisting of an inner core that may be solid and an outer core that may be liquid.

Crater   A steep-sided depression formed after a volcanic vent has exploded or collapsed.

Crevasse   A large, deep crack in the surface of a glacier.

Crust   The outermost layer of the Earth. The continental crust is mostly made of granite and granodiorite; the oceanic crust is mostly made of basalt.

Dip   The angle of a fault, relative to horizontal.

Divergent boundary   The boundary between two tectonic plates that are pulling away from each other or "rifting," making the crust thinner and sometimes creating new crust. Mid-ocean ridges, rift valleys, and volcanoes all occur at divergent boundaries.

Dome mountain   An uplifted mountain that is round or elliptical, with beds dipping away in all directions from a central point.

Drift   All of the sedimentary materials—rock, sand, and clay—deposited by a glacier or its melted ice.

Earthquake   A shaking or vibration of the ground caused by sudden movement of the crust along a plate boundary or fault.

Elevation   The height of a point on Earth, with sea level being zero.

Erosion   The wearing away and movement of rocks and soil by gravity, water, wind, and ice.

Exfoliation   A type of physical weathering where thin layers or sheets of rock are removed from an exposed piece of rock.

Fault   A crack or fracture in rock along which movement has occurred. Movement along a fault can cause an earthquake.

Fault-block mountain   A mountain or range uplifted by normal faults.

Fault plane   The surface of a fault where the two sides of rock meet.

Fault scarp   A steep slope or cliff formed by movement along a fault.

Fault trace   The line of a fault on the surface.

Feldspar   The most common minerals in the Earth's crust (known as aluminosilicates), containing sodium, calcium, or potassium. Clays are formed when feldspars are weathered or exposed to water.

Fissure   A long fracture or crack on the slope of a volcano.

Fjord   A deep, narrow, glacial valley that was flooded by the sea and is filled with saltwater.

Floodplain   The area of flat-lying sediments on both banks of a stream that is covered with water when the stream overflows its banks.

Folded mountains   Mountains that formed when the Earth's crust folded and bent under pressure, often found at convergent plate boundaries.

Folds   Bends in layers of rock, typically found in mountain ranges, ranging in size from microscopic wrinkles to huge arches and troughs 50 miles (80 km)or more across.

Foothills   Lower hills at the base of a mountain range.

Footwall   The side of rock below a fault; opposite of hanging wall.

Freeze-thaw   A type of mechanical weathering when water freezes in the cracks of a rock, expanding the cracks and breaking off pieces of rock.

Frostbite   Tissue damage to body parts caused by exposure to extreme cold.

Geographic Information Systems (GIS)   This is a computer system that can create a map from different sets of geographically referenced data (satellite maps, field observations, and so forth) to help scientists visualize relationships in an ecosystem.

Geologic map   A map that describes the distribution of rocks and soils in an area, including geologic features such as faults and folds.

Geologist   A scientist who studies the Earth, its origins and changes over time, its structure, and the processes that act upon it.

Geothermal energy   A source of energy produced by the heat of the Earth's interior.

Geyser   A hot spring that intermittently erupts a spray of steam and hot water, caused by the release of pressure in an underground chamber filled with hot water.

Glacier   A mass of ice and accumulating snow that lasts throughout the year and flows slowly downhill or out from its center. There are two kinds of glaciers: valley glaciers and continental glaciers.

Global Positioning System (GPS)   A system of 24 satellites that orbit the Earth and make it possible for people with ground receivers to pinpoint their geographic location to within a few feet.

Gneiss   A coarse-grained metamorphic rock, containing quartz and feldspar minerals and exhibiting a characteristic striping or banding.

Graben   A valley formed when the land drops down between two parallel, normal faults in an area where the crust is spreading or pulling apart. Sometimes called a rift valley.

Granite   A coarse-grained igneous rock that contains mostly light-colored minerals and forms much of the continental crust.

Great Rift Valley   A valley produced by stretching of the Earth's crust in the northeastern part of Africa.

Gullies   Small, steep-sided valleys or erosional channels about 3 to 30 feet (1 to 10 m) across.

Hanging valley   A tributary to a U-shaped glacial valley that enters the big valley at a higher elevation, often featuring a waterfall.

Hanging wall   The side of rock that lies above a fault; opposite of footwall.

Headwaters   The source, or upper part, of a river or stream.

Horn   A sharp, jagged peak with many faces, carved by glaciers.

Horst   A long, uplifted block of crust that moved upward between two normal, parallel faults, forming a ridge or plateau.

Hot spot   A volcanic center located within a lithospheric plate, rather than at a plate boundary.

Hydroelectric power   Electricity produced from water power.

Ice age   Long, cold periods in the Earth's history when ice sheets covered a large part of the surface. The last Ice Age ended about 10,000 years ago.

Iceberg   A large, floating chunk of glacial ice.

Ice cap   A covering of ice over large areas of the world's polar regions.

Ice field   An upland expanse of ice and snow.

Ice sheet   A large, flat glacier that flows in all directions from its center.

Ice shelf   A flat stretch of ice that forms when a glacier flows into the ocean.

Igneous rock   A type of rock formed when magma or lava cools and solidifies.

Island arc   An arc-shaped chain of volcanic islands that forms off the coast of a continent near a trench or subduction zone.

Joint   A crack or fracture in a rock where no movement has occurred on either side (unlike a fault).

Landslide   The rapid down-slope movement of soil and rock material due to gravity and the resulting scar on a mountainside.

Lava   Magma that is flowing onto the Earth's surface through a volcanic vent or fissure.

Limestone   A sedimentary rock mostly made of calcium carbonate, which weathers rapidly when exposed to water.

Lithosphere   The outer, rigid shell of the Earth, made up of the crust and the upper mantle.

Magma   Molten (melted) rock beneath the Earth's crust from which igneous rock is formed.

Mantle   The middle layer of Earth, between the core and the crust.

Marble   A metamorphic rock formed by the recrystallization of limestone or dolomite.

Meanders   The winding curves of an older stream or river that develop as it flattens out and erodes its outer banks.

Mechanical weathering   The physical processes by which rock on the Earth's surface is broken up into smaller particles.

Metamorphic rock   A type of rock that is created when igneous or sedimentary rocks are changed or metamorphosed by heat, moisture, and pressure.

Mid-Atlantic Ridge   A mountain range on the floor of the Atlantic Ocean with a rift in its center where magma rises to form new crust.

Mid-ocean ridges   A series of large mountain ranges with rifts on the ocean floor, formed where plates are pulling apart and new oceanic lithosphere is being created.

Minerals   The building blocks of rocks: inorganic substances found in nature, defined by their crystal structures and chemical compositions.

Moraine   A ridge of soil, gravel, and rocks (till) deposited at the sides or ends of a valley that was formed by a glacier.

Mountaineer   A mountain climber.

Mountain range   A row of connected mountains.

Névé   The crystalline or granular snow that has not been compressed into ice on the upper part of a glacier.

Normal fault   A fault where the block of rock above the fault moves downward relative to the block below.

Ocean trench   A long, narrow, deep canyon in the ocean floor that runs parallel to a plate boundary where one tectonic plate is subducting under another tectonic plate.

Orogeny   A mountain-building episode lasting tens of millions of years, during which large areas of crust are folded, thrust faulted, uplifted, and metamorphosed.

Overturned fold   A fold so intense that the oldest rock layers have been bent up and over the top of younger layers, essentially turning the layers upside down.

Pangaea   A supercontinent that broke apart 200 million years ago to begin forming the continents we know today.

Peak   The highest point on a mountain.

Plain   A relatively flat expanse of land without major hills, valleys, or ridges.

Plateau   A flat area of high or elevated land.

Plate boundaries   The borders between tectonic plates.

Plate tectonics   The theory that the Earth's crust is divided into eight major slabs, or plates, and some smaller ones, all of which move independently.

Receding   Moving back.

Rift valley   A long valley formed by the lowering of land between two nearly parallel faults. Commonly found in a divergence zone or other place where the crust is being stretched thin.

Rift zone   A place where two plates are moving away from each other, creating a rift as the crust spreads thin.

Ring of Fire   Zone around the Pacific Ocean where there are many active volcanoes at plate boundaries.

Roadcuts   Walls of rock along the side of a road or highway where a mountain or hill was cut through.

Rock flour   A glacial sediment of finely ground rock.

Schist   A metamorphic rock created under pressure from a sedimentary rock.

Scree slope   A pile of rock debris at the foot of a cliff.

Seafloor spreading   The process that occurs at mid-ocean ridges where plates pull apart and new seafloor is created.

Sea level   The sea's surface, used as zero when calculating the height of a mountain.

Seamount   A mountain rising from the seafloor but not reaching the surface.

Sediment   Eroded particles of rock (sand, gravel, and mud) deposited in seas, lakes, and rivers.

Sedimentary rock   A type of rock formed from the accumulation and consolidation of sediments, usually in layered deposits.

Seiche   A sloshing of water in a lake created by an earthquake.

Shale   A very fine-grained sedimentary rock formed from hardened clay, mud, or silt in thin layers that break easily.

Snout   The forward-most part of a valley glacier.

Snow line   Height on a mountain above which there is always snow.

Soil   The top layer of the Earth's surface, containing rock and mineral particles mixed with animal and plant matter.

Stable minerals   Minerals that are more resistant to erosion.

Strata   Layers of sedimentary rock laid down over time.

Striations   Deep scratches and grooves left on bedrock and boulders by glaciers, showing their direction of movement.

Strike   The angle between true north and horizontal in a fault plane or dipping bed of rock.

Strike-slip fault   A fault along which rocks on both sides move parallel to the strike, rather than up or down.

Subduction   When two plates converge and the heavier oceanic plate sinks, or subducts, under the lighter plate (oceanic or continental).

Subduction zone   The point where a sinking or subducting plate begins to melt as it enters the mantle. On the surface, the subduction zone is characterized by volcanic activity as magma makes its way up through channels in the rock.

Summit   The highest point of a hill or mountain.

Surge   A period of unusually rapid movement of one glacier.

Syncline   A rock fold that arches downward (concave); the opposite of an anticline.

Tectonic   Having to do with the movement and deformation of the Earth's crust.

Tectonic plate   One of a dozen giant slabs of rock that make up the Earth's lithosphere and move independently.

Thrust fault   A low-angle, reverse fault in which the upper block moves up and over the lower block, usually because of compression. The dip of some thrust faults is low and the displacement can be tens of miles.

Tidewater glacier   A glacier that spills into the sea.

Till Rocks and sediment deposited by glaciers, ranging in size from clay particles to boulders.

Topographic map A map showing elevations as well as the positions of mountains, valleys, rivers, and so on, often in color and with contour lines.

Transform boundary The boundary between two plates that are moving sideways past each other in opposite directions.

Tributary glaciers Smaller glaciers connecting with a larger valley glacier.

Triple junction A place where three tectonic plates meet.

Tsunami Large ocean waves, triggered by seafloor earthquakes or volcanic eruptions.

Uplift A broad, gentle increase in elevation.

U-shaped valley A deep valley with steep walls sloping down to a flat floor, eroded into its U shape by a glacier.

Valley Area of low land between mountains.

Valley glaciers Glaciers that flow like slow-moving rivers of ice along well-defined valleys in mountainous areas, often occupying former river and stream valleys.

Volcanic eruption When lava (melted rock) exits a crack in the Earth's crust. Some eruptions are explosive, sending giant clouds of ash, hot gas, and rocks into the air, while some are slower and less dramatic.

Volcanic mountains Formed when magma rises to the surface and piles up over time, forming mountains.

Volcano An opening or vent in the Earth's crust that has allowed magma to reach the surface.

V-shaped valley A valley eroded by a stream or river, whose walls slope evenly (and often steeply) on both sides, forming a V shape.

Weathering The natural processes by which rocks decay and disintegrate.

Bibliography

▲

"About Mauna Kea Observatories," University of Hawaii—Institute for Astronomy Web site. Available online. URL: http://www.ifa.hawaii.edu/mko/about_maunakea.htm.

"About the Terra Spacecraft," NASA Terra Satellite Web site. Available online. URL: http://terra.nasa.giv/About/.

"Active Volcano Hazards," U.S. Forest Service Web site. Available online. URL: http://www.fs.fed.us/gpnf/recreation/mount-st-helens/volcano-hazards.shtml.

Alden, Andrew. "A Hotspot Alternative," About.com: Geology Web site. Available online. URL: http://geology.about.com/library/weekly/aa011401a.htm.

"All About Glaciers," National Snow and Ice Data Center Web site. Available online. URL: http://nsidc.org/glaciers/gallery/mountain.html.

Bailey, Michael J., and Andrew Ryan. "Bradford Washburn, Father of Modern Museum of Science, Dies at 96," *Boston Globe* Web site, January 11, 2007. Available online. URL: http://www.boston.com/news/globe/city_region/breaking_news/2007/01/bradford_ washbu.html.

Bain, Iain. *Mountains and Earth Movements*. New York: Bookwright Press, 1984.

Barnes-Svarney, Patricia L. *Born of Heat and Pressure*. Hillside, N.J.: Enslow Publishers, 1991.

Barovick, Harriett, Nadia Mustafa, and Carolyn Sayre. "Milestones." *Time*, January 29, 2007: p. 18.

"Black Hills Geology." National Park Service—Mount Rushmore National Memorial Web site. Available online. http://www. nps.gov/archive/moru/park_history/geology.htm.

Blauvelt, Harry. "Yes, You Can Snow Ski in Hawaii," *USA Today* Web site. Available online. URL: http://www.hawaiisnowskiclub. com/Mk/UsaTodayMk.htm.

Bramwell, Martin. *Glaciers and Ice Caps*. London: Franklin Watts, 1986.

Brandt, Keith. *Mountains*. Mahwah, N.J.: Troll Associates, 1985.

California Geological Survey—Teacher Feature. "California Has Its Faults." *California Geology* Web site, January/February 1992. Available online. URL: http://www.consrv.ca.gov/cgs/ information/publications/teacher_features/faults.htm.

"Carving History," National Park Service Web site. Available online. URL: http://www.nps.gov/archive/moru/park_ history/carving_hist/carving_history.htm

"Changing Global Land Surface," NASA Terra Satellite Web site. Available online. URL: http://terra.nasa.gov/FactSheets/ LandSurface/.

Clark, Liesl, and Audrey Salkeld. "The Mystery of Mallory & Irvine '24," NOVA Online—Lost on Everest Web site. Available online. URL: http://www.pbs.org/wgbh/nova/everest/lost/ mystery/.

Cook-Anderson, Gretchen. "NASA-conceived Map of Antarctica Lays Ground for New Discoveries," NASA Earth Observatory Web site, November 27, 2007. Available online. URL: http:// earthobservatory.nasa.gov/Newsroom/NasaNews/2007/200 7112725953.html.

Cumming, David. *Mountains*. New York: Thomson Learning, 1995.

Curtis, Neil, and Michael Allaby. *Planet Earth*. New York: Kingfisher Books, 1993.

de La Harpe, Jackleen. "Moon Walk: At the Crater Rim of Mount St. Helens, an Expanse of Ash, Lava, and Smashing Boulders," *Boston Globe* Web site, October 1, 2006. Available online.

URL: http://www.boston.com/travel/articles/2006/10/01/moon_walk?mode=PF.

"Earth," Jet Propulsion Laboratory Web site. Available online. URL: http://www.jpl.nasa/gov/earth.

Exploring the Environment: Rift Valley Fever Web site. Available online. URL: http://www.cotf.edu/ete/modules/rift/rvwhatisriftvalley.html.

"Facts & Figures," Niagara Parks Web site. Available online. URL: http://www.niagaraparks.com/nfgg/geology.php.

Facts About Niagara Falls Web site. Available online. URL: http://www.niagarafallslive.com/Facts_about_Niagara_Falls.htm.

Fagre, Daniel B., and David L. Peterson. "Ecosystem Dynamics and Disturbance in Mountain Wildernesses: Assessing Vulnerability of Natural Resources to Change," USDA Forest Service Proceeding RMRS-P-15-VOL-3, 2000: pp. 74–75.

"Faults and Earthquakes," USGS—Visual Glossary Web site. Available online. URL: http://www2.nature.nps.gov/geology/usgsnps/deform/gfaults.html.

Fortey, Richard. *Earth: An Intimate History*. New York: Alfred A. Knopf, 2004.

"Frequently Asked Questions," Niagara Falls—Thunder Alley Web site. Available online. URL: http://www.iaw.com/~falls/faq.html.

Fry, Carolyn. "Everest's Rocks Reveal Their Secrets: The Summit Was Conquered in 1953, but We Had to Wait 50 Years for the First Geological Map of the Mountain." *New Scientist*, May 31, 2003: p. 14.

"Geographic Information Systems," National Park Service Web site. Available online. URL: www.nps.gov/gis/intro.html.

"Geologic Mapping Product," USGS—National Cooperative Geologic Mapping Program Web site. Available online. URL: http://ncgmp.usgs.gov/ncgmpproducts.

"Geologic Maps," USGS and the National Park Service Web site. Available online. URL: www2.nature.nps.gov/geology/USGSNPS/gmap/gmp1.html.

"Geologic Maps and Mapping," USGS—National Cooperative Geologic Mapping Program Web site. Available online. URL: http://ncgmp.usgs.giv/ncgmpgeomaps/.

"Geologic Provinces of the United States: Basin and Range Province," USGS—Geology in the Parks Web site. Available online. URL: http://geology.wr.usgs.gov/parks/province/basinrange.html.

George, Linda. *Plate Tectonics*. San Diego: KidHaven Science Library, 2003.

"Google Earth," Nature Web site. Available online. URL: www.nature.com/nature/multimedia/googleearth/index.html.

Healy, Donna. "The Night the Mountain Fell: 40 Years After the Hebgen Lake Earthquake, Memories Are Still Fresh," *Billings Gazette* Web site, updated August 15, 1999. Available online. URL: http://www.billingsgazette.com/magazine/990815_mag01.html.

Heezen, Bruce, and Marie Tharpe. "The Great Rift Valley Will Lead to the Somali Plate," *Plate Tectonics* Web site, September 25, 2007. Available online. URL: http://www.platectonics.com/oceanfloors/somali.asp.

"History," U.S. Coast Guard-International Ice Patrol Web site. Available online. URL: http://www.uscg.mil/lantarea/iip/General/history.shtml.

"Hotspots: Mantle Thermal Plumes," USGS—This Dynamic Earth Web site. Available online. URL: http://pubs.usgs.gov/gip/dynamic/hotspots.html.

"How Earthquakes Happen," USGS—Earthquakes Web site. Available online. URL: http://pubs.usgs.gov/gip/earthq1/how.html.

Huntington, Sharon J. "How Do You Map What You Can't See?" *Christian Science Monitor*, February 1, 2005: p. 18.

"Ignorance: The Main Reason Behind Deaths on Mount Everest," MedIndia Web site. Available online. URL: http://www.medindia.net/news/view main print new.asp.

"Introduction to Geologic Mapping," USGS—National Cooperative Geologic Mapping Program Web site. Available online. URL: http://ncgmp.usgs.gov/ncgmpgeomaps/geomapping.

Johnson, Rebecca L. *Plate Tectonics*. Minneapolis, Minn.: Twenty-First Century Books (Lerner Publishing), 2006.

Karlinsky, Neal. "Hikers Go Inside Mount St. Helens," ABC News Web site, July 31, 2006. Available online. URL: http://abcnews.go.com/print?id=2208305.

Kentucky Geological Survey. "Did You Know That Pine Mountain Has Moved?" University of Kentucky Web site. Available online. URL: http://www/uky.edu/KGS/education/pinemountain.html.

Lamb, Simon, and David Sington. *Earth Story*. Princeton, N.J.: Princeton University Press, 1998.

Leary, Warren E. "Mapping the Earth, Swath by Swath." *New York Times*, January 25, 2000: p. F 1.

———. "New Map of Antarctica Brings Frozen Landscape Into Focus." *New York Times*, December 4, 2007: p. F2.

"The Long Trail of the Hawaiian Hotspot," USGS Web site. Available online. URL: http://pubs.usgs.gov/gip/dynamic/Hawaiian.html.

Lye, Keith. *Our World Mountains*. Morristown, N.J.: Silver Burdett Press, 1987.

"Managing Fragile Ecosystems: Sustainable Mountain Development," United Nations Division for Sustainable Development Web site. Available online. URL: http://www.un.org/esa/sustdev/documents/agenda21/english/agenda21chapter13.htm.

Matz, Mike. "Volcanoes, Volcanoes, Volcanoes: Iceland Is One of the Most Eruptive Places on Earth," Science Wire Web site. Available online. URL: http://www.exploratorium.edu/theworld/iceland/volcanoes.html.

"Mauna Kea," USGS—Hawaiian Volcano Observatory Web site. Available online. URL: http://hvo.wr.usgs.gov/volcanoes/maunakea/.

"Mauna Kea, Hawaii," VolcanoWorld Web site. Available online. URL: http://volcano.und.nodak.edu/vwdocs/volc_images/north_america/hawaii/mauna_kea.html.

"Mission," NASA Earth Observatory Web site. Available online. URL: http://earthobservatory.nasa.gov/masthead.html.

"Mission," U.S. Coast Guard—International Ice Patrol Web site. Available online. URL: http://www.uscg.mil/lantarea/iip/General/mission.shtml.

"Mission Overview," Jet Propulsion Laboratory—Shuttle Radar Topography Mission Web site. Available online. URL: http://www2.jpl.nasa.gov/srtm/missionoverview.html.

Morris, Neil. *Earth's Changing Mountains*. Chicago: Raintree, 2004.

——. *The World's Top Ten Mountain Ranges*. Austin, Texas.: Raintree Steck-Vaughn, 1997.

Mount St. Helens: The Victims of the Eruption Web site. Available online. URL: http://www.olywa.net/radu/valerie/mshvictims.html.

"The Mount St. Helens Ten Essentials," U.S. Forest Service Web site. Available online. URL: http://www.fs.fed.us/gpnf/recreation/mount-st-helens/ten-essentials.shtml.

"Mountain Glaciers," National Snow and Ice Data Center Web site. Available online. URL: http://nsidc.org/glaciers/gallery/aster_bhutan_mtn.html.

Oxford University Press. *Planet Earth*. Oxford: Oxford University Press, 1993.

Pearce, Fred. "Global Warming: The Flaw in the Thaw." *New Scientist*, August 27, 2005: p. 26.

Pearce, Jeremy. "Bradford Washburn; Led Landmark Mapping of Grand Canyon," obituary, New York Times News Service, as printed in *San Diego Union-Tribune* Web site. Available online. URL: http://signonsandiego.com/uniontrib/20070121/news_lz1j21washbur.html.

"Plate Tectonics: The Mechanism," University of California Museum of Paleontology Web site. Available online. URL: http://www.ucmp.berkeley.edu/geology/tecmech.html.

"Plate Tectonics and People," USGS Web site. Available online. URL: http://pubs.usgs.gov/gip/dynamic/tectonics.html.

"Plate Tectonics and Sea-Floor Spreading," USGS—Cascades Volcano Observatory Web site. Available online. URL: http://vulcan.wr.usgs.gov/Glossary/PlateTectonics/description_plate_tectonics.html.

Press, Frank, and Raymond Siever. *Earth*. San Francisco: S.H. Freeman and Company, 1978.

Reasoner, Mel, Lisa Graumlich, Bruno Messerli, and Harald Bugmann. "Global Change and Mountains." International Human Dimensions Programme (IHDP) on Global Environmental Change: Update. January 2002. Bonn, Germany: IHDP.

Salkeld, Audrey. "Irvine—The Experiment," NOVA Online—Lost on Everest Web site. Available online. URL: http://www.pbs.org/wgbh/nova/everest/lost/mystery/irvine.html.

——. "Mallory," NOVA Online—Lost on Everest Web site. Available online. URL: http://www.pbs.org/wgbh/nova/everest/lost/mystery/mallory.html.

Sauvain, Philip. *Mountains*. Minneapolis, Minn.: Carolrhoda Books, 1996.

Schwartz, Jerry. "Ninety Years After the *Titanic*, the Ice Patrol Guards Against Icebergs," The Glacier Society Web site. Available online. URL: http://www.glaciersociety.org/press/AP050902press.htm

Science in Africa. "Africa Is Being Torn Apart—Proof of Continents on the Move." Available online. URL: http://www.scienceinafrica.co.za/2007/february/continents.htm.

Scott, Michon. "Observing Volcanoes, Satellite Thinks for Itself," NASA Earth Observatory Web site, December 6, 2007.

Available online. URL: http://earthobservatory.nasa.gov/Study/VolcanoSensorWeb/.

Silver, Donald M. *Earth: The Ever-Changing Planet*. New York: Random House, 1989.

Simon, Seymour. *Mountains*. New York: Mulberry Books, 1994.

Simonson, Eric, Jochen Hemmleb, and Johnson, Larry. "Ghosts of Everest," Outside Online Web site. Available online. URL: http://outside.away.com/outside/magazine/1099/199910mallory1.html.

"So You Want to Climb Mount St. Helens?" Mount St. Helens National Volcanic Monument Web site. Available online. URL: http://www.fs.fed.us/gpnf/recreation/mount-st-helens.

"Steam Explosions, Earthquakes, and Volcanic Eruptions—What's in Yellowstone's Future?" USGS Web site. Available online. URL: http://pubs.usgs.gov/fs/2005/3024/.

Stone, Lynn M. *Mountains*. Chicago: Children's Press, 1983.

"Topographic Map," How Products Are Made Web site. Available online. URL: http://www.madehow.com/Volume-4/Topographic-Map.html.

"Topographic Mapping," USGS Web site. Available online. URL: http://erg.usgs.gov/isb/pubs/booklets/topo/topo.html.

UN News Service. "Climate Change Threatening Mountain Ecosystems," December 11, 2007. Available online. URL: http://www.un.org/apps/news/printnews.asp?nid=25021.

"Understanding Plate Motions," USGS Web site. Available online. URL: http://pubs.usgs.gov/gip/dynamic/understanding.html.

USGS—Aerial Photographs and Satellite Images Web site. Available online. URL: http://erg.usgs.gov/isb/pubs/cooklets/aerial/aerial.html.

"USGS Contributions to the Climate Change Science Program: Glacier Studies," USGS—Global Change Research Web site. Available online. URL: http://geochange.er.usgs.gov/poster/glacier.html.

Venables, Stephen. "Bradford Washburn: A Life of Exploration." *Geographical*, January 2005: p. 89.

Walker, Sally M. *Ice on the Move*. Minneapolis, Minn.: Carolrhoda Books, 1990.

"Water Resources," The Mountain Institute: Why Mountains Web site. Available online. URL: http://www.mountain.org/mountains/whymtns.cfm?slidepage=water.

"Welcome," U.S. Forest Service Web site. Available online. URL: http://www.fs.fed.us/gpnf/mshnvm.

"West Yellowstone Quake Lake," West Yellowstone Traveler.com Web site. Available online. URL: http://www.westyellowstonetraveler.com/features/quake.shtml.

"What is a Geologic Map?" USGS–Geology in the Parks Web site. Available online. URL: http://geology.wr.usgs.gov/wgmt/aboutmaps.html.

"Why Map the World With Radar?"Jet Propulsion Laboratory—Shuttle Radar Topography Mission Web site. Available online. URL: http://www2.jpl.nasa.gov/srtm/whymaptheworld.html.

"Why Mountains?" Global Mountain Program Web site. Available online. URL: http://www.globalmountainprogram.org/AboutMountains.htm.

"Why Mountains?" Mountain Research Initiative (MRI) Web site. Available online. URL: http://mri.scnatweb.ch/content/view/20/54.

"Yellowstone Caldera, Wyoming," USGS–Cascades Volcano Observatory Web site. Available online. URL: http://vulcan.wr.usgs.gov/Volcanoes/Yellowstone/description_yellowstone.html.

"Yellowstone's Quiet Power," University of Utah Web site. February 28, 2007. Available online. URL: http://www.eurekalert.org/pub_releases/2007-02/uou-yqp022807.php.

Zoehfeld, Kathleen Weidner. *How Mountains Are Made*. New York: HarperCollins, 1995.

Further Reading

▲

Collier, Michael. *Over the Mountains: An Aerial View of Geology*. New York: Mikaya Press, 2007.

Harris, Tim. *Mountains and Highlands*. Chicago: Raintree Publishers, 2003.

Hartemann, Frederic V., and Robert Hauptman, *The Mountain Encyclopedia*. Lanham, Maryland: Taylor Trade Publishing, 2005.

Macdougall, J.D. *A Short History of Planet Earth: Mountains, Mammals, Fire, and Ice*. New York: John Wiley, 1996.

Mountains from Space: Peaks and Ranges of the Seven Continents. New York: Harry N. Abrams, 2005.

National Geographic. *Our Dynamic Earth* (video). Explains the theory of plate tectonics and includes live footage of earthquakes and volcanoes. Washington, D.C.: National Geographic Society, 1979.

Patent, Dorothy Hinshaw. *Shaping the Earth*. New York: Clarion Books, 2000.

Price, Martin F. *Mountains: Geology, Natural History, & Ecosystems*. Osceola, Wis.: Voyageur Press, 2002.

Rhodes, Frank Harold Trevor. *Geology*. New York: St. Martin's Press, 1991.

Staub, Frank J. *America's Mountains*. New York: Mondo Publishing, 2003.

Vogt, Gregory L. *The Lithosphere: Earth's Crust*. Minneapolis: Twenty-First Century Books, 2007.

Woodhead, James. *Earth's Surface and History*. Pasadena, Calif.: Salem Press, 2001.

WEB SITES

Canadian Broadcasting Corporation "Geologic Journey"
http://www.cbc.ca/geologic/eg_rockies.html
Online video documentaries take viewers on a spectacular geologic tour of the Rockies, the Appalachians, and the Canadian Shield.

Earthmaps
http://www.earthmaps.com/index.html
Links to animated Web sites that show what happens below the Earth's surface, including magma movement and the formation of metamorphic rocks.

Exploring Earth "Geologic Features of Mountain Belts"
http://www.classzone.com/books/earth_science/terc/
content/investigations/es1101/es1101page04.cfm
Photographs of folds, faults, igneous rocks, and other geologic features of mountains.

Franklin Institute "Earth Science Hotlist"
http://www.fi.edu/learn/hotlists/geology.php
Online resources for learning more about the geology of the Earth, including a site designed by elementary students.

The Mountain Institute "Learning About Mountains"
http://www.mountain.org/education/subexplore/explore02.
cfm
A good explanation of how mountains are made and sculpted, plus links to animated Web sites showing the birth of the Himalayan mountains and how new crust is formed at mid-ocean ridges.

National Snow and Ice Data Center "All About Glaciers"
http://nsidc.org/glaciers/gallery/mountain.html
Photographs of different forms of glaciers around the world and a good explanation of how glaciers advance and retreat.

United States Geological Survey (USGS) "Ask-a-Geologist"
http://www.walrus.wr.usgs.gov/ask-a-geologist/
Browse the FAQs (Frequently Asked Questions) to learn more about geology, earthquakes, volcanoes, and more.

University of California Museum of Paleontology "Geology—Plate Tectonics"
http://www.ucmp.berkeley.edu/geology/tectonics.html
A good overview of the evidence that led to the theory of plate tectonics and global animations of continental drift from 750 million years ago to the present.

University of Leeds "Dynamic Earth"
http://www.see.leeds.ac.uk/structure/dynamicearth/index.htm
Full-color animations of plate tectonics, the structure of the Earth, and the continental collision that formed the Himalayas.

USGS "What on Earth Is Plate Tectonics?"
http://www.geology.wr.usgs.gov/parks/pltec/index.html
Illustrated text describing the Earth's crust, core, mantle, and plate interactions at convergent, divergent, and transform boundaries.

USGS and National Park Service "Plate Tectonics Animations"
http://www2.nature.nps.gov/geology/usgsnps/animate/pltecan.html
Animated illustrations of plate movements and boundaries from the U.S. Geological Survey. Also links to "U.S. Geology in the Parks," with geologic maps and descriptions of rock types and geologic time.

Picture Credits

▲

Index

▲

About the Author

▲

CAROLYN ARDEN would rather be hiking in the mountains than sitting at a desk. She writes about science from Westport, Connecticut, where she lives with her husband, two daughters, a dog, and two rabbits. She credits her love of the outdoors to her mother, who spent lots of time exploring nature with her children. Arden started collecting rocks when she was 10 years old. She studied geology at the University of Illinois, spending her senior year summer at field camp in the Bighorn Mountains of Wyoming. She married her husband, John, on Signal Mountain in Moose, Wyoming, overlooking the magnificent peaks of the Teton range. After earning a master's degree in journalism at Northwestern University, Arden worked for *Outside* magazine and the Chicago Academy of Sciences. She is now a freelance writer and author of children's books. She thanks her loving family for their support and dedicates this book to her mother, Marilyn, who loved the Earth and all its wonders.